I0823702

HEAD OF HOUSEHOLD

OLIVER MUNDAY

SIMON & SCHUSTER

NEW YORK AMSTERDAM/ANTWERP LONDON
TORONTO SYDNEY/MELBOURNE NEW DELHI

Simon & Schuster
1230 Avenue of the Americas
New York, NY 10020

First Simon & Schuster hardcover edition February 2026

Interior design by Kyle Kabel

Manufactured in the United States of America

1 3 5 7 9 10 8 6 4 2

Library of Congress Control Number: 2025944821

ISBN 978-1-6680-7830-3
ISBN 978-1-6680-7832-7 (ebook)

For Lillian

When you look at a quiet, dull life, like my parents' good life here, cursorily and from a distance, you think—what could be better?

—Ivan Turgenev, *Fathers and Sons*

CONTENTS

FISTS

Walt was disappointed to know, after passing the nicer resort, that they'd be staying at the lesser of the two. Since Claire was five, he'd planned these father-daughter trips—typically escapes from the Brooklyn winters. They'd gone to Miami, Vieques, Mexico, and this year to Curaçao. Vacations used to be points of excitement for Claire, but now she was a prickly fourteen-year-old who seemed, at best, to endure his presence.

The shadows of the attendants and the potted plants were stark against the stone of the resort's entrance. The late-morning heat baked Walt in his sweatshirt. He grabbed their bags from the back of the bus. Claire looked up from her phone, her slender sunglasses glared by the sun. Her shoulders were pale from months indoors.

"Why're you still wearing a hoodie?" she asked.

"The bus was cold."

Though Walt couldn't see her eyes, he knew they were partially drawn in skepticism or annoyance or some other microclimate of disgust. He wouldn't change into his mesh shorts and T-shirt until they got settled in the room; he'd spent the last eight months doing CrossFit and eating clean and dropped thirty-five pounds. He was fitter than he'd been since his late twenties preparing for his wedding. Claire seemed only to register his errors, but she might be impressed to see him shirtless on the beach. He wanted his newfound strength to be legible.

Their room was small, two queen beds and an outdated TV mounted on the wall. The air from the AC was a relief. Walt changed after putting his clothes away in the closet. He offered to unpack for Claire, but she lay on the bed, typing furiously on her phone with her glasses tilted up on her head. A strand of blond hair hung on either side of her face. She smiled to herself, which Walt took to mean: boys.

"Want to go for a walk?" he asked.

"I'm gonna chill a bit first, OK?" She barely looked up.

He knew better than to press so early in the trip. His wife, Lucy, had warned him to control his temper. He should give their daughter a grace period, to allow her to *unfurl*, as she described it. She'd be less testy that way.

The beach was a short walk from their room, the Caribbean a blue impossible to capture with a photo, though he'd tried in many selfies with Claire over the years. Couples sat drinking from punctured coconuts or sharing an early cocktail in one of the many kidney-shaped pools overlooking the ocean. Walt walked out to the cabanas and found a chair, taking off his shirt in the shade. In Brooklyn, he'd started to compare himself to the many soft-bodied dads at the indoor pool where he took his son for lessons. At his last tally, there were only two men fitter than he was (apart from the instructors). To see the many paunches testing the elastic limits of faded bathing suits, the erratic patches of back hair, made Walt feel superior in his fitness.

The sun sent a shiver down his triceps and his back once he stepped into it. His shadow against the sand was lean and angled, an italicized character. He flexed his arms and pulled his shoulders back, watching the curves take shape. The contours made him look strong. A passing woman might find him sexy—if not outright, then at least for a dad who had decided to give his body one last shot at desirability before death.

He pulled his phone out and flipped the camera, lifting his hand to capture his torso in the frame. He walked through the sand to find a more ideal angle of light, and a tan woman in a turquoise bikini sat up on her beach chair nearby and noticed him. Walt flipped the camera back around and walked to the water to take photos of the ocean instead.

On his way back to the room, he peeked in the window of the Kidz Club—one of many amenities the resort offered to parents. A group of kids of various ages sat around drawing, watching TV, and playing Connect Four. A shaggy-haired boy who looked too old to be there sat in a beanbag chair in the corner scrolling on his phone. His presence was strange.

Claire walked up to Walt then. "Don't be a creep," she said, looking into the window with him.

"I'm just curious," he said.

She'd changed into her bathing suit and wore her big Phoebe Bridgers T-shirt over it. "I need an iced latte."

"You and me both," he said.

Her sandals slow-clapped along the tiles as they walked to the lobby café. When Walt stepped up to the counter to order, a dour woman in a white polo carrying a clipboard came over and stopped him. She pointed at the sign prohibiting bare feet. Walt looked down, and then back, noticing the tracks he'd left.

"Really," Claire said, embarrassed.

"What?" he said. "I didn't realize . . ." He turned to retrace his steps, which made it more of a spectacle. Like he'd been caught in a trespasser's trap.

In the afternoon, they went to the buffet, housed in a large open room with ceiling fans that failed to dissuade flies. Claire's plate was a pie chart of beige: fries, tortilla chips, and a small roll. The only thing more frustrating than her metabolism was her complete unappreciation of its ability to destroy carbs.

"What shall we do tonight?" Walt asked. "I saw they're doing karaoke-bingo at the main pool."

"Dad. Lame."

"Kidding. Jesus."

A woman sat down at the table next to them, joined by a teenage boy. Walt recognized him from the Kidz Club.

"As far as buffets go, this one really isn't bad," the woman said to them.

"Food is so mid," the boy said. His voice was deep.

Claire chuckled to herself. Walt smiled. "We just arrived," he said.

Claire chewed her roll carefully, staring back down at her plate.

"Just the two of you?" the woman asked.

Walt nodded. "My wife is on a trip with our nine-year-old, Daniel." He looked at Claire, hoping to encourage her to talk. "We take a father-daughter trip every year."

"So sweet," the woman replied. Her arms were toned, and she was dressed in athleisure, her dark hair pulled back in a ponytail. "My husband is off working. Always." She rolled her eyes. "I'm Angela, and this is Cory," she said.

Walt introduced himself and Claire.

"I think I saw you in the Kidz Club earlier?" Walt said to Cory.

Claire widened her eyes at her dad. Jutted her jaw.

"Yeah," Cory said. "It's dumb, but it's OK to chill there sometimes. The trampoline is fun." He scooched his chair out a bit. "Claire, you should come."

Walt was surprised by the directness, maybe also impressed. Cory had dark brown hair and fine features; his slim nose was reddened by the sun. His shoulders were broad. Walt wondered how attractive Cory was to girls his age, how much he could bench. *Don't obsess*, he told himself.

Claire feigned laughter.

"Seriously," Cory said. He looked at Walt then. "It'd be fun."

Walt eyed him before Angela cut in.

"Unlike you," Angela said, "maybe she wants to spend time with her dad." Angela palmed her son's arm, warning Cory not to eat too much. She said her husband would be disappointed at dinner.

"It's like he's not even on vacation with us," Cory said, almost to himself.

Angela looked at Walt. "My husband can be very particular," she said.

Soon after, they got up to leave. "Enjoy the rest of your day," Angela said. "I'm sure we'll run into you two again."

That night, Claire and Walt had an early dinner. Walt sat opposite her, twisting the base of his glass against the tablecloth, which tussled in the wind. The sun was setting.

He remembered how Claire used to collect stuffies from each destination they'd been to.

"I miss how you used to line up your stuffed animals on your bed."

"That was so many years ago, Dad." She eyed her phone. Again. "Ugh, I miss my friends."

Walt turned indignant. "They're all on vacation too. Besides, you've made a new friend and we've barely been here a day."

Claire shook her head. "This place is grimy."

"Expensive, is what it is." He conjured Claire's formerly tiny face, back when she was a year old, one of her first times at the ocean. She'd gotten sand in her eye and no matter how hard Walt blew, one tiny granule remained. He drew his finger as close as he could without touching her eye, barely making contact, and the grain was gone. Just like that: the satisfaction of having lifted it away.

He'd meet her where she was. "So what do you think of Cory?" he asked.

"I don't know—he seems fine?" She reached for her facedown phone and turned it over.

"Better or worse than the boys at school?"

"Cory is *not* cute."

Walt was relieved, somehow. He sipped his drink. "I'm glad we still do these trips," he said. "I'm excited to lounge on the beach together."

Claire looked up. "Mom texted me to remind you to put on sunscreen."

"*Dead*," Walt said, the same way Claire and her friends did.

She laughed and smiled. "OK, that was actually good."

Before dessert, Claire was tired and wanted to go to bed early. Walt decided to grab a drink at one of the bars by the pool. A large man in a tank top tilted back the last of his beer. He looked mildly perturbed, or pensive, and for some reason Walt thought this was Angela's husband. He could recognize the posture of a dad who'd stepped away from his duties, apart from his wife, for a moment to himself.

Walt ordered a lager. He ran his thumb against the callused ridge of his palm, a satisfying reminder of his progress with pull-ups. He imagined a woman approaching him without pretext and setting her spare room key down beside his drink, allowing the scenario to play out until he spooked and retreated to the safety of his life.

The man near him set his glass down on the bar, resting his big fist beside it. Some workout routine had helped the man develop massive forearms.

"The gym here isn't great," Walt said.

The man huffed and grinned without answering, pulling out his phone.

Walt eyed the peaks and valleys of the man's jagged knuckles. When Walt was a kid, his dad had played rough. He'd come up with a game where Walt would try to bite his dad's fist. His dad would rotate his large fist back and forth, trying to prevent the bite, his knuckles turning against Walt's small teeth. So unnatural, yet satisfying. Like trying to devour a rock.

When the man at the bar finally stepped back, he moved his empty glass close to Walt. Walt thought he was coming over to join him. But a younger woman with a netted pink top approached and hugged the man, grabbing his biceps. The man smiled, catching Walt's eyes before they walked off together.

The next morning, Walt woke to the pixelated resort logo on the TV and momentarily forgot where he was. Claire wasn't in her bed. He flexed and rubbed his stomach, feeling the abs that were present yet only barely visible through a thin layer of fat. He wanted to get out on the beach with Claire, to reveal his new body, but then his head throbbed. The night before he'd had a third beer at the bar, a caloric excess he'd allow himself only on vacation.

He put on trunks and a new T-shirt and opened the sliding doors. The air was crisp, the sky empty of clouds. The sun deepened his headache, and when he went back in the room, he couldn't find his sunglasses. Claire had set an extra pair of hers out on the nightstand—a bright white—and he grabbed them.

He bought two lattes, showing his flip-flops to the officious woman who'd scolded him the day before. As he left, he noticed something dart across the grass at the footpath. He stopped and scanned the ground and then, after peeling his eyes, saw the iguana. Its size was shocking. He kneeled to look, staring at the granular, almost digital pattern of the reptile's skin. Its claws were like grappling hooks. The creature remained completely still until its gullet flickered and it turned its scaly head. Walt watched the tiny black seed of its eye before it waddled away.

On the beach, two kids sat beyond one of the cabanas. He walked closer to find one was Claire, her hair jumping in the breeze. The other was Cory, who was shirtless. Walt was annoyed; he thought to turn around and go back to the room, but Claire had already noticed him.

"I didn't know where you'd gone," Walt said, walking up. "I come bearing coffee."

"I ran into Claire in the lobby earlier," Cory said. "I was at the gym." As he leaned back, his abs contracted into a shell. It was almost like he was holding a flex for Walt; Walt tried not to stare. This fucking boy and his unearned musculature, his stomach like the tide had rolled out and left ripples in the sand.

Claire looked up. The reflection of Walt's body warped in the dark lenses of her glasses. "What the hell," she said. "Why're you wearing my glasses?"

He'd forgotten he had hers on. "I couldn't find mine."

"You look like op Kurt Cobain," Cory said.

Claire hung her head. Walt just stood there, tensing.

Cory got up, shading his brow from the sun, his bicep hardening. He was nearly as tall as Walt. "Just playing," he said. He pushed Walt's arm with unexpected force and some coffee dripped on Walt's hand. "The fem thing works for you."

Claire's laughter was harsh; Walt handed her the latte. Cory reached out his hand as well, and Walt thought he was joking. After a second of standing there, he handed Cory the coffee.

"I think we're gonna get breakfast, and then maybe go to that club," Claire said.

"I thought we were going to the beach." Walt wanted to tell her that he'd already gone to the shack to reserve snorkeling gear.

She dilated her eyes to plead with him.

"Just text me," Walt said. "Don't make me come looking for you."

"Yay—thank you." Claire lifted her glasses and looked at him. "And, Dad—leave my glasses in the room, please," she said. "You look insane."

Only two other people were working out in the resort's gym. A stale scent hung in the air. Walt watched himself in the mirror, hanging from the pull-up bar. He rose and his shirt rode up, exposing his carved hip bones under the light. The sight surprised him. At CrossFit the only mirrors were in the bathroom, so he never saw himself during a workout.

On the elliptical machine in the corner, a man sweat profusely from his forehead with a towel around his neck. He had starkly dyed hair and wore reading glasses, with a page of the *Financial Times* folded against the monitor. Maybe *this* was Angela's husband. There was something menacing about his normality—the baggy gray shirt and small shorts—like it concealed an extreme anger or sinister sexual aptitude. He'd unleash a barrage of threats at Angela, or yoke Cory up for breaking curfew.

When the man was done on the elliptical he came over to the pull-up bar. "Can I jump in?" he asked. He had a southern accent, which surprised Walt.

The man hoisted himself up. He easily finished ten pull-ups, which was impressive. After he jumped down, Walt stepped up and reached to grab the bar. The man held his arm out stiff at Walt's unflexed stomach. Walt clenched his jaw and stared at the man.

"Sorry," the man said, "can't waste that momentum."

He began to swing and heaved himself up over the bar like a gymnast. Walt watched him, wanting to swiftly kick him in the chest on his downswing. He balled his hands, squeezing tightly. Why was he obsessing, again? He turned away and noticed the water fountain. He walked over to it, glancing over his shoulder, and then jabbed the wall. Relief, then the throbbing. As he sipped the water, the cold on his teeth distracted him from the pain in his hand. As Walt left, the man across the room had already moved on to leg lifts.

Late the next morning on the beach, Walt saw Angela wading in the surf in a broad sunhat. A sheer cover wrapped her hips. He and Claire had slept in late, which seemed a waste since they were heading back home the day after next.

Walt grabbed two spare lounge chairs and set their stuff down. Angela waved to him from the water. Cory was skipping rocks beside her.

Claire took off her T-shirt to reveal a bikini Walt had never seen: stark black and white stripes that vibrated like an illusion. He couldn't remember the last time he'd seen so much of her body—he almost flinched. The tiny hairs along Claire's legs flared in the light as she walked down to the water. Walt grabbed his phone to text Lucy about the swimsuit's provenance. He wanted to fight against the instinct he knew to be rooted in misogyny, to believe even some of the body positivity mantras he'd lobbed at Claire. Lucy would convince him it was only a bathing suit.

He watched Cory and Claire, with their lithe adolescent bodies, ease into the water together. If he was honest, he'd tell her she was lucky and that she should embrace the comfort she felt in her body before it became a crucible to maintain.

Walt removed his shirt and wiped some lotion across his midsection. He pressed his fingers into his skin, reminded himself of his muscles again. He felt almost naked.

A moment later Angela came over. "I hope Cory isn't overwhelming you," she said.

"No, not at all." Walt smiled. He was relieved she'd noticed. "I'm glad Claire has a friend. She might actually return home with good things to say about this trip."

"Cory has been out of school this year," she said. "I haven't seen him like this in months. Your daughter has a glow about her."

When the breeze splayed Angela's cover against her thigh, Walt saw that she was bruised. It was faint, like the stain left by a watercolor brush soaked in a napkin.

He looked away. "Ah, I'm sorry to hear it. Is he OK?"

"Generally, yes, but this is the third school we've tried him in. We just decided—or I decided, my husband was very opposed—that it would be good to give him a break. All that change is traumatic."

Walt nodded, wondering whether this meant Cory was violent. "Where's your husband today?"

She laughed to herself. "In some conference room on Zoom. He never stops. Better this way. The sun isn't kind to him. He's bald and burned his head badly the first day we were here."

So the pull-up star wasn't her man.

"You're a gym rat, too, huh?" she said.

Walt smiled and turned bashful, looking down at himself and fiddling with the string on his trunks.

Angela pointed at his pile of stuff on the chair. "You've got the ridiculous gym key this place insists on."

Walt was mortified. "Someone's got to make use of the sullied yoga mats and dumbbells."

Claire and Cory came up to them, both dripping wet and dappled in light. Claire pointed at Walt's midsection. "Gross," she said.

A flash of heat spread across his cheeks. He looked down. He'd failed to fully rub in a swipe of lotion.

"Can Cory and I hang out tonight?" Her tone was conspicuously sweet then. "There's a party on the beach later."

"It's the only one they do here that's not lame," Cory said.

Angela smiled to herself.

"Claire, come on," he said.

"Not late—just for a bit?" Claire asked.

Angela looked away.

"Please." Claire stepped near him, and the chill from her arms reached his.

"We're getting dinner first," Walt said. "And you need to be back by eleven. No exceptions."

Claire beamed. "Of course!"

When the kids walked away, Angela grabbed his forearm, said how sweet he was with Claire. Walt detected a note of pity in her voice, or judgment, as if he were letting Claire get away with too much. Angela thought he was soft. He imagined her bald husband holding himself above her on the bed. Up on his knuckles like an ape. Maybe her bruises were from his large hands, gripping her thighs. Maybe she came hardest from this dominance, and maybe this dominance was never as clearly defined to her as it was when talking to men like Walt.

Dinner with Claire lasted barely forty-five minutes, like he'd exceeded her internal time limit on proximity to him. On the flight over, she'd fallen asleep on his shoulder, her large headphones pressing into him, and he relished the near comfort of it, the distant bass in his ear. It was the best he'd get.

Walt bellied up to the bar again. Torches were lit along the perimeters of the pools. On the beach, in the distance, he could see the beginnings of a bonfire, a man in some kind of vest lugging a conga drum across the sand. He beat his fist steadily on the bar top.

Walt ordered a mescal from a bartender with wide hips and tiny spandex shorts. He watched her as he sipped it slowly. He and Lucy hadn't slept together in six weeks. Before that it had been a month. Walt couldn't tell whether she found him more attractive because of his new body. It was as if she thought he was quieting an internal crisis, one that was fine so long as it remained contained. All he wanted was for her to look at him again through the feral eyes of her youth.

A warmth crept across his body. He gulped the rest of his drink and ordered another. There had been a recent TikTok trend that Claire's friend had posted, a panning video of her dad with his glasses perched on his head, making dinner in the kitchen. The text on the video read: *My dad says he used to fight the women off.* After a lingering shot of the unassuming father, several old photos flashed of a much younger man, with chiseled jaw and tousled hair. Had any of Claire's friends made comments about him—thought he was hot? He'd sometimes wear a workout shirt around them, subtly pulling back and flexing his shoulders. He thought of the man, earlier in the gym, halting him. Walt's heart quickened.

He finished his drink and ordered a double. He looked out at the beach, trying not to check for Claire. There was a small shack with a pool table, where Walt had gone to reserve the snorkels they hadn't used. People were going in and out to join and rejoin the bonfire.

His legs were unsteady when he left the bar and headed back to the room. Along the way, he glanced across the grass looking for the iguana, which he'd yet to see at night. How did it sleep, how did the spray of long spikes lay when it was not alert, when no one watched? It would be easy to sneak up and grab its neck, to squeeze. *Stop, stop*, he told himself. What did it even fucking matter?

Walt woke with his hands folded against his chest. He was drunk, disoriented. Outside, the window showed mostly black—a distant orb of light. He grabbed his phone; it was after midnight. Claire wasn't back. His wife had texted him to say that he should hang in there, that they'd be home soon. He was confused, as if Claire had shared something with Lucy that she hadn't with him.

He'd been explicit about Claire's curfew; an hour late was egregious. He called her and her phone didn't ring, but went straight to voicemail. The Wi-Fi signal was spotty. He took a breath to calm himself, wishing he'd exchanged numbers with Angela earlier.

He got up and rinsed his face and tried Claire again without luck. His head felt heavy. He put on flip-flops and a sweatshirt, steadying himself. Outside, it was chillier than before. The dark palms swayed. He walked quickly to the pools and scanned the beach as the remains of the bonfire glowed. A shirtless man, seated in the sand, sipped a Red Stripe. Walt began to worry, but the worry then yielded to anger. He walked the length of the main pool area, dodging busboys carting glasses into the kitchen. At the shack with the pool table, two women were wiping down tables.

"Have you seen a girl—fourteen, blond? She was with a boy with dark hair?"

They both shook their heads, grinning at each other. "Maybe ask the concierge?"

What had Cory done? Walt headed to the beach, deciding to trace the resort's perimeter back to their room. He couldn't believe Claire's flagrant disregard, endangering herself. This would never have happened were Lucy here; Walt pictured Daniel, his son, who so rarely disrespected him. The thought only gave his anger more definition.

As he neared a cove of rocks, he noticed two bodies on the beach. He hustled to get closer. The wind whipped at him, blowing his hood against his head. He saw Claire. Her arm was splayed on the sand, and Cory was crouching over her. Walt froze. He watched the slow movement of Cory's head. It looked then like Claire's arm was pinned down. Claire's hand, nearly balled, looked helpless in Cory's grasp. Then Claire reached up and palmed the back of Cory's neck.

But earlier, she'd told him . . . Walt hit his foot hard against a rock hidden in the sand. The pain was acute and instantaneous and ran up through his body. He tucked his bottom lip between his teeth and bit down hard, furthering the feeling. He started to shake with frustration that all at once vibrated into a rage. Then he was off, running through the pain. Cory noticed him before Claire did. She screamed as Walt pulled her away, her voice shrieking in his ear. *Daddy*. He mounted Cory's shirtless body, pinning him to the ground. Cory got an arm loose and struck Walt's jaw with the heel of his hand. He flailed and flung sand into Walt's face, his mouth. Walt spat and regained control using his weight and his knees. Walt had him. He was stronger than the boy, much stronger. But as their eyes caught, this wasn't enough. Cory winced and couldn't pull free. Walt punched him once, and then rose to hit him with more force. Again. And again. That Cory had given up still wasn't enough.

From twenty yards down the beach two barefooted men sprinted toward them, sand exploding from their heels. They passed Claire, who was still on the shore. She watched through blurry eyes as her dad finally stopped and collapsed onto Cory. The intimacy of their bodies would haunt her. She felt the urge to go to her dad's side, but couldn't.

GUTTER BALL

The bowling alley had a distinct yet unplaceable smell—stringent, foamy—one that made Ben feel like he was inhaling someone else's nostalgia. Neon lights staggered through the semi-darkened space. Several arcade games and toy machines bleeped. It wasn't even 10:00 a.m.

A man's voice came over a loudspeaker. Ben's head throbbed and he could still feel a fatty streak in his throat. He'd tried to avoid coke last night but, once he realized he'd be leaving the party without the warmth of a woman at his side, he'd sniffed several bumps and kept it moving.

"There are a few classes here today, so we need to mind our manners," the large man said. "A few ground rules before you hit the lanes." His voice was gruff, that of a Brooklyn Italian of simmering onions and garden Virgin Marys. He outlined the shoe etiquette (sneakers fine!) and safety precautions. "Also, I haven't had my second cup of coffee yet, so be nice."

Their yellow school T-shirts bright beneath their coats, the kids bobbed and swayed, failing to form a line against the wall. Ben found Amelia, grinning back at him as she balanced on one foot. His smile pained his temples. He needed Advil. Or a coma. He'd been running late to meet the class at school and hadn't had time to stop for any. The other three chaperones, all moms from Amelia's kindergarten class, were surprised to find him as their fourth volunteer.

One woman gave Ben a flaccid wave.

"Hey," he croaked.

"Late night?" she asked.

Amelia's teacher, Ms. Kraus, double-checked her small notepad and placed a hand on Ben's forearm.

"You'll be with Amelia, Tyler, Eugene, and Mary. Lane five."

Her sudden touch made him alert. Traces of lemon lingered from her damp curls.

She crouched to meet the kids. "Give Mr. Ben your coats and we can get ready to play!" He remembered the way she'd grinned at him during pickup weeks before. The thin eyeliner below her eyes. Her tight hoodie. She'd encouraged him to come on the trip, said she looked forward to whooping him. Each afternoon she smoothed a tiny sticker on the back of Amelia's hand, her thumb brushing it back and forth.

Amelia put her palms in Ben's. "Ewwww, Daddy! Your hands are sweaty."

He wiped them along his pants. "They're not," he said. "They're fine." He was warm now, but his body hadn't started dripping yet. He needed water.

"I wanna show Tyler the flip trick, Daddy." Amelia grabbed his hands again.

The thought of activating his midsection so that she could crawl up his body and flip backward made him want to puke. He did it anyway, pushing himself further into discomfort.

Once she'd landed, Tyler bumped her, vying for position.

"I want to do that too," he said.

That Tyler had a bowl cut annoyed Ben more than the fact that he was an asshole. "*One* time," Ben warned.

Tyler was heavier and his shoes pressed hard against Ben's flannel shirt, steps that made Ben want to drop him. Tyler landed and almost fell back before steadying himself. He stood defiantly and kicked his foot in the air. "These are Yeezys."

"No they aren't," Ben said. They were plainly Air Force 1s.

"They are. My mom told me."

"Whatever you say, champ." Ben mussed Tyler's hair.

Tyler swatted away his hand. "Don't call me champ."

Marcy, another chaperone, came over as several kids hovered near the ball cradle.

"Make sure you keep an eye on them. Their hands can get pinched between the balls."

Ben stared at her, puerile jokes flooding his mind. How many nuts had she crushed in her day?

He nodded, eyeing her Phish shirt beneath her blazer. Beside them, Ms. Kraus set out stout bottles of water on the tables for the kids who didn't bring a thermos. Ben was parched and wanted to grab one and gulp it. When a bottle fell over and rolled off the edge, Ms. Kraus bent to pick it up. He eyed the glorious curve of her ass.

"You OK?" Marcy asked.

"Yeah—why?"

"Your nose is bleeding."

He reached up and felt the wetness: crimson drips on his fingers.

"I'm fine."

He turned away from the kids and wiped his sleeve against his face.

"It's happened since I was a kid."

She pulled a pack of wet wipes from her pocket and he took one grudgingly. He'd always meant to have them for Amelia. Ben cleaned his face and stared at the faint pink strokes on the wipe. The smell sent a brief rush to his head.

"I've got more if you need them," she said.

"I should be good unless someone decides to take a run at me."

On the digital screen hovering above the alley, Ben's name glowed in all caps. Despite the playful shit talk with Ms. Kraus, he hadn't bowled since his twenties. He and his ex, Tina, had been set up by mutual friends, their first date at a bowling alley. She'd beaten him and he'd gotten drunk and leaned over the table to kiss her. She had whispered *I owned you* under her breath, and he had felt almost delirious. They'd always talked about going bowling again, but he never could bring himself to visit the site of their originating passion.

At the lane, Ben poked his fingers in the first two holes of the nearest ball. His thumb traced the rim of the bottom hole, without entering. He cupped the ball in his palm, carefully wound up, and then flung it with impressive force. It glided down the center of the slick corridor and the pins exploded in a snarl. Two remained upright, almost touching.

"Yay, Daddy!"

A few of the kids clapped. Ben was almost embarrassed, as he turned around, by the effort he appeared to have put in. Ms. Kraus raised an eyebrow and tucked her hair behind her ear.

"*OK*, Mr. Ben." She nodded at the remaining pins. "How will you handle what's left?"

"With aplomb." He'd never spoken that word before, and doing so made him suddenly confident.

Ms. Kraus crossed her arms and pursed her lips. Ben went over, grabbed a new ball, and held it against his stomach. Entering Ben's periphery, Tyler stepped in front of him. Ben wanted to shoo him away with a leg.

"It's Daddy's turn!" Amelia marched over and confronted Tyler. He swatted her hand away and grabbed her other arm.

"Stop." She frowned at Tyler and furrowed her brow exaggeratedly.

Ben beamed at her resolve. Tyler looked shocked by the severity in her voice, which was enough to prevent Ben from stepping in.

When Ms. Kraus came over, Amelia's eyes suddenly welled. She sank into her teacher's arms. "Tyler—remember the invisible bubble," Ms. Kraus said. "We don't need to touch."

She settled both kids and then squatted to watch the lane with them. Ben took one last look at Amelia on her knee, Ms. Kraus's hand gently belting Amelia's waist. He extended an arm and flung the ball, this time with spin. It swung wide, almost hitting the bumper, but veered back toward the pins. He clenched his fists. It just nicked the pin on the right. One remained, alone in the center, before the metal arm came in and swept it away.

An hour hadn't yet elapsed and some of the kids were already sprawled on the benches, stretching out like drug fiends. Ben understood their waning energy. When he'd gone to the bathroom and sipped from the faucet, he'd leaned his head against the porcelain and closed his eyes. He just needed to prove himself a competent enough chaperone so that word might reach Tina, and maybe her attorney. He'd make some headway in securing more than one sleepover a week with Amelia.

Tyler headed to the lane to take his turn. He heaved the bowling ball up to his shoulder and tossed it in a shot-putting motion. The ball hit the bumper. Ben winced.

Amelia's legs dangled from the seat as she ran her teeth along her bottom lip, which she did when she was shy or chastened. She'd been quiet since the fracas with Tyler. Ben would tell her in private that she should never let a little prick like that get under her skin, wield that kind of power over her.

Pretending not to see her, Ben walked by before slowly and dramatically tripping and falling over. The movement churned his stomach and strained his headache, but he sensed Amelia's smile even before he heard her laugh.

Tyler stood by the machine, absentmindedly rubbing a ball as he watched the neighboring lane. Ben then noticed the next ball being fed in and heading toward Tyler's hand. No one else was paying attention. The ball moved incrementally closer. It knocked into place without a sound, trapping Tyler's chubby fingers. He tore them away and turned to see if anyone had noticed. He met Ben's eyes. For a second it appeared he was deciding whether to cry, trying to make sense of Ben watching. Then Tyler screamed.

Ben crept over.

"You're OK, buddy. Tell me what happened."

He spoke slowly and rubbed the boy's bony shoulders.

Tyler couldn't speak through the tears dripping down his cheeks. At first he tried to shrug Ben off, but then he settled. He grabbed his bright red fingers in a bundle, as if holding something that didn't belong to him.

Amelia looked worried. Marcy, in her still stupid blazer, glared at Ben. Ben felt hot and sick, a little gleeful that no one had seen Tyler get hurt. Amelia had a hand at her lip as she watched Tyler leaning against Ben. "Is he OK, Daddy?"

"He'll be fine," he said. "He's a tough guy."

Ben bit the nozzle of Amelia's unicorn thermos and sucked one last gulp, a fleeting quench.

"Hey!" Amelia said. "That's mine!"

He set it back down and took off his flannel shirt, hung it over the seat.

"I'm sorry. I was thirsty, dude!"

"Those aren't for grown-ups, Daddy."

As Ben leaned against the table, Ms. Kraus came over with her phone to take pictures.

"Come on, guys," she said. "No one's too cool for photos."

Ben looked at Tyler and forced a smile. He imagined Tina seeing this picture in the shared class folder for the trip.

Ms. Kraus glanced at Ben's arms, the fine dark lines of a ship. "I didn't realize you had tattoos."

He rubbed his arms and felt a chill. "Only a few," he said.

"Can I see?"

"Of course."

She stepped closer. Her hair's smell swept across his nose, not as intense as it had been earlier.

He lifted his sleeve and flexed his tricep. He eyed the rosy swipe on his wrist from his bloody nose.

Tyler craned to look too. "Rainbows are for girls," he said, a dumb smirk now lazing on his face. Ben was so relieved to be raising a girl in moments like this, much as he anticipated Amelia's teenage years bringing disaster.

"Real men love rainbows, champ."

Ms. Kraus traced the arc of the rainbow with her finger, the teal of her nail a more saturated version of what showed on his skin. Amelia's name was in a scroll beneath.

"This is quite possibly the sweetest thing I've ever seen," she said.

Her sentiment aroused him.

"Does Amelia love it?"

Amelia had seemed indifferent when he got it, later amused. "You inked up too?" Ben asked.

"I've got one." She smiled. "But I keep it hidden."

During the next game, one of the kids in Ben's lane skipped a turn, which threw off the rotation. The scores were a shambles, but no one cared. Ben leaned back on the bench and scanned the rest of the alley, the other three parents so engaged. He'd always been a fuckup, but sometimes he was a charming one. Tina was an IP lawyer, and her friends saw her dating a filmmaker as proof she wasn't a square. Ben made the occasional hazardous choice—namely drugs—because Tina thrived when taking care of him, even seeming to draw vitality from it. But this had changed once Amelia was born. Tina's patience with him buckled just as his patience with caretaking did. He grew even more lazy and unhelpful. Spiteful. After the separation, Ben's superego proved to be an even shittier chaperone than he was. But being a father, a co-parent, required a renewed focus to protect the most fragile thing in his life. He wanted Amelia to be sleeping at his place more often, but he was overwhelmed by the work of making a home for her. He was struggling financially after Vans had pulled their sponsorship out of what was supposed to be his second feature documentary (following skaters in Cuba). A vice president had been fired, and Ben's guaranteed two-year salary had vanished. He was scraping by with freelance, doing tedious production work to afford the small studio close enough to walk to Amelia. His lawyer was unduly expensive, which was all the more painful because in the end he'd be the one receiving child support.

When Ben opened his eyes, he found Tyler standing in front of him.

"Can I sit on your lap?" The boy's face verged on a smile, which came across as menacing to Ben.

Ben looked around. Amelia was playing with the other kids at the edge of the lane. Ms. Kraus was near enough to see.

"Fine," he said. He hoisted Tyler up onto his knee.

"Do you live with Amelia?" Tyler asked.

"I don't. Not anymore." Ben began bouncing his knee, and Tyler giggled. "Why do you ask?"

"She says she only lives with her mommy now," he said. "My dad works late. He's not home sometimes. He's a UPS driver."

Ben imagined himself hauling packages in those brown shorts. They had a strong union and potential six-figure salaries. "Do you ever ride on the truck with him?"

"He says I'm not allowed. But I have a toy truck just like it. He gave it to me."

Ben's knee began to tire. A vile burp was trapped in his throat. "Do you miss Amelia when you're not with her?" Tyler asked.

"Of course I do."

"My dad always tells me he misses me."

"Did Amelia tell you that she misses me?"

"She said sometimes her mommy and daddy squabble. That she's going to have two homes." This glimpse of his daughter's private conversations made Ben wonder about her budding inner life.

He lowered his knee and guided Tyler off, but the boy continued to talk as he stood in front of him. "What toy does Amelia have to remember you when you're gone?"

Ben couldn't think of one that was unique to him. Tina had bought all of her favorite toys.

As the game wound down, Ben asked Marcy to keep an eye on his lane while he went to get water. He wandered to the bathroom, passing a grabber machine with only several drab animals at the bottom. None of the machines seemed to be working, but when he came out again, he desperately wanted a Sprite.

He opened his wallet to a dark, diamond-shaped cavity.

Ms. Kraus came around the corner, surprising him. "Thirsty?"

"Machines don't take cards," he said. "I'm dying for a Sprite."

"In case you hadn't noticed, this alley was airdropped from a 1980s Midwestern exurb. It's been eerily preserved."

He chuckled.

"You should be drinking water," she said. "But here." She reached into her back pocket, and Ben tried not to look at her ass again, but there it was. His heart began to beat as she unfolded the money.

He fed the two bills into the slot, saying he'd pay her back. She rolled her eyes and then looked through the dingy plexiglass beside him. "So curious about your choice here. I feel like it will tell me a lot."

"I'm a simple man," he said.

"I took you for a Coke head," she said.

He felt stymied to have drugs in his system. "Sprite's the only soda that holds up in plastic."

When the drink tumbled out, he kneeled to grab it. Ms. Kraus's denimed waist was only inches from his nose. He wanted to hook his pointer finger through her belt loop and pull her close.

As he stood, he uncapped the bottle and took a sip. The bubbles frothed along the inside of his jaw.

"I've been meaning to ask you something," she said.

He was excited to be in her thoughts.

"Would you want to do a morning reading with our class? You seem so comfortable with the kids, and I think they'd enjoy it."

"Sure." He was disarmed that she'd noticed this aspect of his character.

"I want to give the parents a chance to get more involved. Amelia would lose her mind if you came."

She palmed his forearm. Again. Ben thought briefly of the nearby bathroom's privacy. His heart continued beating like a kind of summons. Without looking, he stepped toward her, dropped the bottle to the floor, and put a hand at her waist, easing her up against the machine. He closed his eyes and soon felt something at his lips. Her finger entered his mouth sharply.

"What the fuck are you doing?" she said.

A second later, Amelia rounded the corner. She looked surprised to see them standing by the machines.

Ben stepped away from Ms. Kraus.

Marcy followed behind. "Amelia needed to pee and couldn't find you."

Amelia's eyes darted from Ben to Ms. Kraus. She looked confused by Ms. Kraus's face, leveled in shock.

After a second, Ms. Kraus reached out her hand to Amelia. "I'll take you, sweetie."

Ben leaned to pick up the Sprite, bound to erupt the next time it was opened. Amelia didn't look for him as she walked off.

"We should get back out there," Marcy said. "The kids are wildly outnumbering us."

"Right," he said. His mind focused on the motion of his missteps. He wanted to stay and wait for Amelia, but Ms. Kraus would return with her. He followed Marcy back to the lanes.

As they prepared to leave, Tyler was trying to do the sturdy dance (which Ben knew from Instagram); it looked Russian as he bounced along the hardwood floor. Amelia watched him, without smiling.

Ms. Kraus spoke loudly. "OK." She raised one finger up above her head, and the kids alerted to the signal. "Let's find our partners and form a line. The grown-ups will get your coats and then we'll put them on quickly. Capeesh?"

Capeesh, the entire class yelled back.

Ben grabbed the small jackets from a nearby hook. The closer he looked, the more he realized how dirty Amelia's pink puffer was. He should try to clean it, or have it cleaned. He should buy her a new one.

Ms. Kraus was close, helping a student with their jacket.

"I was completely out of pocket and crazy," he said. "I didn't get much sleep. I'm so sorry . . ."

She spoke sternly, without meeting his eyes. "Don't."

Ben felt pitiful, standing there reprimanded. Like another kid in her class. He rolled up his shirtsleeves. He imagined a filled sink soaking the threads of his plaid—the black and red, the dried blood from his nose—and what color the water would be once the shirt was wrung out.

She moved past him in the crowd, taking care not to brush his body.

Ben realized in that moment that he didn't know how old Ms. Kraus was. It was possible, according to the humid fugue of his mind, that she was closer in age to Amelia than to him.

On the bus, Amelia and Tyler had figured out how to buckle themselves in without Ben's help. He sat in the row behind them and rested his head against the leather. Ms. Kraus walked by, silently counting the students. He watched her teal nails; she'd wiped away her lipstick.

Tyler stuck out his tongue at Amelia as the bus lurched forward and jolted them. She would typically laugh at something like that, but instead she turned away.

Ben stared from the window as the bus turned the corner on a residential street. In the front yard of a small blue house, an empty stroller sat beyond the steps. His focus made him feel sick. He and Tina had viewed this place on Zillow; he remembered the deco numbers and the orange door. They'd had that stroller for Amelia once. Where was it now? The entire scene had been an idea, though he wasn't sure if it had ever been his. It suddenly occurred to him that he hadn't had a new thought since the divorce, and that his entire life as a dad had been a series of reactions to the thoughts of others. The forward movement of time had been incidental. He wanted to puke.

Tyler continued grasping for Amelia's attention. He leaned his face close to hers and bared his clamped teeth.

"Stop," Amelia said.

Tyler refused to listen. He wagged his head back and forth, making a dull noise with his mouth.

Amelia lunged at him. A second later, Tyler screamed. Ben rose in his seat and saw a bite mark on Tyler's forearm, little streaks of Amelia's saliva tracing it. "Hey, you two," Ben said. He turned around and saw the nearest chaperone. *They're fine*, he mouthed. He rolled his eyes.

"She bit me!" Tyler said.

Ben shushed him; Tyler wiped tears from his face.

"She didn't mean to," Ben whispered. He brought Amelia to sit beside him. She remained still without saying anything. He peeked over at Tyler, rubbing his little arm. "We'll get you some ice at school. You'll be OK." Ben grabbed the Sprite from his seat and handed it over. "Don't tell anyone."

Tyler took the bottle. Ben pulled Amelia up onto his lap. He felt her heart racing. Her breath was a little tart from the candy they'd had. He remembered the first time he'd smelled her breath's scent rather than simply feeling its warmth. He'd imagined that something inside of her had cracked, a new gas seeping out. There was no stemming it now.

VANDAL

That his name is Jason has ceased to matter. He would love, simply, to go by Dad, or Daddy, but since her third birthday weeks ago, Carrie has been stubborn—or dedicated, depending on the angle—and he has been Steve. Only Steve. He was mortified by the comparison to a goofy kids' YouTuber who seemed only to get balder and pudgier in each new clip. But he gave up protesting once he realized Carrie's commitment was hitched to his frustration.

It is early—always early. Light sprays in through the living room window, misted with dust, turning the old wood floor golden. Jason shuts his eyes against it. He imagines the sun as a tiny hole in a faraway nozzle.

His wife, Hannah, is asleep in the next room; every room in their small apartment is the next room. Since Carrie was nine months old, Jason has been the one to get up with her each day and watch her until the nanny arrives. Hannah's job as a PR strategist is demanding, more important and more lucrative than his. The morning is his shift, his half of the parenting peace agreement. A trial of not counting down the minutes.

"Da—" Carrie catches herself. "*Steve.*" She pauses, leaning over to reach beneath the couch and grab the new toy that her aunt, Hannah's sister, sent her recently. A light-up drawing board that's impossible to clean. "Let's draw."

"Draw—now?"

She smears a strand of hair away from her face with the heel of her hand, holding out a peach-colored marker.

He sits up, regretting his question. "Of course we can. What should we draw?"

"*You* draw something." Carrie jabs the marker at him.

She flicks the background light off and on. She stares at his hand. He uncaps the marker, puts the tip against the board, and quickly picks it back up.

"Please? Steve?"

He stares at the black board once more. Streaks are smudged along the plastic. He thinks of the lewd doodles he used to draw in school textbooks but begins drawing the curved line of a bird. The proportion of the head is too small.

"What is it?" she asks.

"Nothing," he says. He wipes the line away and stops short of drawing something else.

On the living room couch, during sleepless nights, Jason is limited to activities that don't require light, lest the glare reach through the gaps in the blackout curtains on Carrie's French doors and wake her. This has never happened, but in the unlikely event that it does he would be fucked.

He lets an arm hang from the side of the couch. He feels a pull across his chest, a reminder of exercise, a reminder he ignores for fear of the logistical effort required. He thinks about listening to music or skimming the news on his phone's dimmed screen, but he's bored by both. On the floor, beneath his knuckle, he feels something smooth. He grazes it—a marker from Carrie's drawing board. He lifts and twirls it gently between his fingers, eyeing the slender beam of plastic in the dark.

Turning to lean half off the couch cushion, the blood rushing slowly to his head, he reaches down and pulls out the drawing board. He won't turn its light on, of course, but his eyesight has adjusted. The surface looks clean, though he knows it's not, the way concrete walls in the city sometimes appear pristine at night. When he was fifteen, he loved how an alley wall looked under moonlight: the fine grain of concrete or coarse mortar, the scent of spray paint filling his nose. When he'd first started writing graffiti, he'd used latex gloves to hide the traces. Eventually he stopped because he enjoyed the constellation of color on his fingers the next morning. Loved scratching it away. If he was out tagging long enough, he could pick flecks of color from the hairs in his nose.

Jason uncaps the pen. The letters flow out seamlessly. The word is more familiar even than his signature: *Moat*. He follows the angled line from *M* to *o*, the *o* as it swoops to form a lowercase *a*, tracks the tail of the *a* as it runs up to form the *t*, a final connection that had taken months to master. Jason observes the tag in wonder—his tag—unwritten in more than twenty years. When he was a teenager the word was arbitrary; the beauty of the tag was how each letter connected. It is, now, he thinks, more precise and more refined than it used to be. What he's written is orchestrated and alive. He's impressed by his mind's retention. The muscle memory.

He gets up from the couch and creeps to the bathroom, board under his arm, pen in hand. Carefully, he shuts the door; the toilet seat is cold through his briefs. He turns the board's light on, imagining a billboard along a highway, lighted under a heavy sky, a blank wall freshly painted. Fear had ruled him once—fear of police, of rival graffiti writers, of those who were fearless—but now he remembers the speed with which he'd looped those shiny black letters along a wall, a roof, a mailbox.

He wets some toilet paper and begins to scrawl and wipe, scrawl and wipe. He fills the board, which is not so dissimilar from how he spends his days; as a production designer tracing his pen against a digital tablet, enhancing the work of others. But this is different. He's astonished at how unthinking it is to get his tag down, though *getting up* is the term of art.

Jason hears a noise beyond the closed door. Turning his head to listen, he goes still. He sees a shadow move along the wall through the door's frosted glass. Then a knock.

He panics. "I'm in here."

"Are you OK?" Hannah's voice is muted through the door.

"I'm—" Maybe she imagines him masturbating, but sitting on the toilet with his daughter's drawing board is somehow worse, more alarming. "Almost done," he says. He watches her blurry form.

"I need to pee."

"One sec." Jason turns on the faucet and lowers the board carefully into the tub. He will retrieve it in the morning when he's up with Carrie.

He opens the door and smiles at Hannah. Her new haircut, much shorter and brushing her chin, reveals more of her neck and shoulders. As he attempts to inch past her, she reaches out and grabs his forearm. She pulls him back and kisses him with barely parted lips. His eyes close reflexively.

"I'm gonna wash," she says. "Wait up for me."

In the bedroom, the floor is cold beneath his feet. He finds a condom on a shelf in the headboard. The blood inside of him is a bifurcated stream pumping to his heart and his groin.

Hannah comes back into the room naked, leans over her side of the bed to search for lubrication. Since giving birth, she's used the cream as a sexual expedient. It's no fault of his, he has decided, but one of biology.

He tries not to watch her, wary of imposing additional pressure on her and ruining the mood. Each second is immense, and his focus on the floor disrupts his desire. He reaches slowly to the bed, grabs a pillow, and covers himself. The dense stitching from one of the pillow's petals grazes his penis.

"Wait," Hannah says.

He clenches the pillow tighter, trying to sustain his erection.

"Fuck," she says. "Fuck," tossing the empty tube back into the bin. She falls, on her side, to the bed.

He is shocked by the volume of her voice. He watches a loose ripple of skin form along her ribs. His condom slips, slightly, from its wilting erection.

"We can still try?" She turns over to look up at him with large eyes.

He sits on the bed with the pillow on his lap, just as he had with the drawing board moments before.

"What?" she asks, palming his arm.

"Nothing." He is wary of further failure.

"Jason, I'm trying."

That her effort needs underscoring annoys him. That effort is needed at all. Arousal, like anger, should be pure and instantaneous, should it not? He knows this belief isn't fair. But he still pulls away.

From the next room comes a noise, which may mean Carrie's awake. He listens but hears nothing more. Hannah gets up and walks into the dark kitchen to open the fridge. She grabs a small container of orange juice as the light hits her bare thighs. She swigs the drink and her lips glisten with pulp.

Outside it's raining. The sound on the back of the AC unit is harsh. Somehow, when it pours, the apartment feels even smaller. Jason stares at Carrie's nude torso, her belly button a chickpea. He's on all fours; Carrie wants to ride him around the living room like a horse.

"Steve," she says. "Go down."

He wonders which fate is worse—the horse's or Steve's. The answer, of course, doesn't matter. He will be both. He will be anything she needs him to be.

Her hands are warm on his neck, her weight a solace. Once, when she was eighteen months old with a high fever, he'd sat with her in a rocking chair as she'd slept across his chest for hours. All he'd had to do was hold her.

"Giddy-up!"

As they round the corner to the kitchen, they hear cautious knocking at the front door. Carrie breathes in dramatically. Jason is relieved at the distraction as she dismounts. They approach the door down the hallway in mock suspicion.

"Dada Jason, what's up?" It's Tony, their upstairs neighbor. His hair is long, tied in a ponytail, and his beard is dense. Both are dark. Tony's son, Markus, younger than Carrie by three months, is behind Tony in the lobby of the building. Markus appraises the many scooters and bikes parked below the staircase. Carrie runs out the door, yelling his name repeatedly.

"We're going to the warehouse. You two want to join?"

Tony's warehouse, where he runs a small delivery company, is a spacious option for entertaining the kids on rainy days. Jason enjoys Tony's spontaneity, the cavalier way he keeps the kids entertained.

"Check with the boss?" Tony jokes, jutting his chin at the apartment behind Jason.

"You already got clearance, huh?" Jason says. The two chuckle.

This Saturday morning, Hannah would be grateful for a few more hours of sleep. The weather on Jason's phone reports rain all day. "Give me a few minutes to pack up," he says.

Jason knows Tony's name isn't really Tony from the labels on his Amazon boxes in the lobby. Tony is from Kyrgyzstan, awaiting full citizenship. He speaks English with a heavy accent, but very well. Tony's wife, an Albanian woman, has Americanized his name for convenience, though she hasn't done the same for herself.

They ride to the warehouse in Tony's van, which Markus and now Carrie refer to as the *broom broom*. Jason does not own a *broom broom* and has been reminded lately of the need for a *broom broom* by both his wife and his daughter.

"Look, Steve." Carrie points out the window.

Through the dripping pane is the water tower rising in the distance. Carrie notices it every time they're on the expressway. The first time she'd seen it she'd described it as a toy rocket.

"The water tower, Markus," she says. Markus sits up in his car seat, yells out in recognition. Tony turns his head and grins through puffs from his vape.

The warehouse is cold. Water leaks from the corners of the ceiling, a patchwork of wood and corrugated metal. Carrie is enticed by all the foreign materials and devices—brackets, shiny clamps, and bolts the size of flashlights. A pile of pale two-by-fours rests beside a shelf, and Jason thinks of the sled Tony built Markus last winter. Long and sturdy with curved, cradled seats. Jason had taken Markus and Carrie out to a hill one school-canceled, snowy afternoon and was stopped by envious parents holding their kids' flimsy saucers.

On the bottom shelf, Jason spots a shallow box of spray paint cans, covered by a translucent tarp. He bends down and traces a finger along a can, the curved, rusting edge of metal. It's the famed brand of cans he'd used as a kid, the ones he'd bought with allowance while claiming, to his friends, to have stolen.

"So much paint," he says.

Tony steps up. "We had to make custom shipping containers." His voice is deep, raspy. "A wealthy customer wanted his shipments in black boxes, large black boxes. Spray paint was easiest. We spent weeks building them. He's loyal so I don't ask."

Jason stands slowly. His hips are weak.

"You want it, old man?" Tony nudges the box of spray paint with the toe of his boot. "We haven't used them since." Whenever Tony notices Jason noticing something, he offers it to him. This is true regardless of price or apparent worth. In just the last month it has meant a VR headset and an antique midcentury chair. Jason imagines these gestures pertaining to Kyrgyzstani culture somehow, an old-world traditionalism, because they're distinctly un-American.

"No, I . . ." Jason pauses. "I used to spray-paint—write graffiti—when I was younger."

"The Soviets hated graffiti in my country," Tony says. "My brother used to write his name on his bed frame over and over, drove my parents crazy." He smiles at the ground, shakes his head as he does whenever he invokes his younger brother, after whom Markus is named. "Why did you stop?"

The honest answer strikes Jason as weak, or at least something that Tony would consider weak. Writing graffiti is risky in every sense; kids he knew growing up had been jumped and jailed for it. "It's childish, I guess."

"That's bullshit," Tony says.

"Maybe," Jason says.

"You know Baudelaire? Genius means retrieving childhood at will. You should continue."

Typically, Jason would've laughed off Tony's advice, thought it facile, but he'd invoked Baudelaire. Jason must now read Baudelaire to catch up.

Tony claps his hands. "Who wants to see magic?"

The kids dance in tight circles saying *me*, *me*, *me*. Tony gives them both earplugs that look like candy corns. He fits safety goggles around their small, round heads. He warns them to stand back—Jason, surprisingly, too—as he lowers a circular blade's teeth onto a piece of pipe. Tony is making the best of what's at hand, reveling in it, even.

Sparks spray as smoke rises from the metal. Carrie's eyes are glossy, the sparks reflected in her goggles slipping along her pupils. She leans forward, hands on her knees, and the sparks just miss her skin.

"It makes sense," Hannah says. "Financial sense."

It is late—always late—and she has been offered another promotion at her consultancy. She and Jason sit on the bed, not facing each other but side by side. They are both turned toward the wall, as if waiting for something to be projected onto it.

"I'm asking you to be open."

It's true that they would save money if Jason cut back further at work or went part-time in earnest; they could let the nanny go and Jason could pick Carrie up from preschool in the afternoons.

"Money can't be the only reason," he says.

"Why're you so attached to your job all of a sudden?"

His attachment isn't to the job itself but to the distraction it offers. He was never supposed to be a production artist for ten years. Working for an ad agency had been a stopgap.

"You want to live in this box forever?" she asks.

"We're lucky to live here." His voice rises. "We used to be in love with it."

He turns to the window, the magnolia tree waiting to bloom in someone else's yard. Maybe he's not ready, just yet, to think about moving, or buying a house, with the same degree of urgency. His would not be a future of his own making.

"We need more space." She crawls her fingers toward him. "And besides, Carrie loves being with you. She'd be lucky to learn from you right now."

"I barely have any freedom left to give up." He feels pathetic having to plead with her.

"You'd be doing it for us."

Is he selfish? he wonders. He remembers, when he started going back to work after paternity leave, how Monday mornings began to feel like Friday nights with all they promised.

"In six months we'll have a down payment, sooner with this raise."

He is losing this negotiation, he can feel it. He was losing even before he opened his mouth. Though he knows she's trying to be considerate, she rubs his bare thigh in a way that feels infantilizing.

"You'll have your moment."

"So you at least understand the moment isn't now." He is impatient, angry. "Don't dangle the hope of some improved future moment in front of me." There is an echo of the conversation they'd had after two years at the ad agency. Sacrificing for later, later being *now*, which has proven insufficient.

Carrie is perched on Jason's shoulders, her tender calves in his grip. They exit the apartment, and she reaches to grab a metal pole in the scaffolding above. He adjusts his balance under the motion of her shifting weight.

"Steve," she says, twisting again, "it's Markus!"

Tony's van is double-parked down the block. The hazards are flashing, the sliding door open. Markus sits alone, feet dangling from the runner, eating jelly worms. This means Carrie will soon be joining him.

"Where's Dada?" Jason asks Markus.

"He'll be right back." Markus holds a yellow and green worm in the air, slick and chewed. Carrie reaches for it.

Tony calls out sweetly to Carrie as he approaches the van. He and Jason bump fists. "Get in your seat, Markus."

Jason doesn't want to walk today. "Can we hitch a ride?"

Usually he sits in the back of the van with Carrie, but today she's OK on her own.

Tony drives, puffing his vape. "Markus isn't getting enough at this school. We've been building robots at home and then he goes to school and builds forts with foam blocks. I want more for him."

"It's preschool, as long as they're kept alive I'm good with it."

Tony shakes his head and grins. After dropping the kids off, Tony says he wants to show Jason something. They return to the van, and Tony offers to take him downtown to work after the detour. At the foot of the passenger seat, Jason notices the cans of spray paint. The labels are shinier than before. Jason thinks that maybe Tony has cleaned them. He lifts one up and inspects the tiny ribbed cap, rests his finger on the groove.

Tony instructs Jason to bring the cans with him as he parks. They pass Tony's warehouse, rounding the corner through an alley. Tony opens a door the color of clay.

"My neighbor," Tony says, then takes another pull from his vape. "He's a set designer, but he left the space early. Said I can use it for another month or so. They will scrub the place after we're done."

The space is vast, its walls smooth concrete, blank except for a few notations and measurements marked in wax pen.

"Show me," Tony says, nodding his head at the wall.

"Show you what?"

"I want to see how you do it."

"Here?" Jason demurs. "You're sure it's OK?"

Tony's laughter is raucous. It is almost cruel as it echoes. Jason crouches beside the cans like a golfer gaming out a putt. He lifts one, shakes it, and the ball inside clacks against the aluminum. The sound sends a chill across his arms, his neck. He's forgotten how close to stand. He runs his palm across the surface, rubbing dust between his fingers. He sprays a quick black line. The smell is sharp.

He remembers, then, the spray caps he'd ordered from a graffiti magazine when he was a kid—the bright ad offering a seemingly unending variety of nozzle widths. The night after the caps had arrived, he'd snuck out to a nearby bridge that had been closed for construction. He'd realized he had to return home, after hours of filling the bridge's hulking concrete columns, only when he saw the neon vest of a construction worker showing up as the sun rose.

He turns to look at Tony. He takes two steps back.

"What does it say?" Tony asks, tilting his head.

"'Moat.'"

"Like a castle?"

Jason nods.

Tony crosses his arms. "How did you come up with that?" he asks. "It's kind of sophisticated, for a kid."

It had felt accidental to Jason. "I liked the way the letters looked together."

"So keep going," Tony says. "Decorate your castle."

Jason proceeds. He holds the cap down and slows his hand, allowing drips to form; splays the cap out for fat, diffuse letters. Each *Moat* possesses its own quality, a distinctness amid the apparent uniformity of the pattern. A row emerges and Jason wants to fill the entire wall, floor to ceiling. The way surfaces take on a new meaning once they're available to him—he'd forgotten.

Running out to grab a ladder from his warehouse, Tony is eager to facilitate. Jason then works vertically, slowly, to fill the upper portion of the wall. When Tony heads back outside to talk to one of his drivers, Jason realizes he's now late for work. The project manager had called out his tardiness two weeks before, but Jason felt artists deserved to arrive on their own time. He doesn't bother pulling out his phone to email. He will ask for forgiveness rather than permission.

He stops, moving the ladder aside. He walks backward to take in his effort. He stands alone in the center of the space, blurring his eyes and focusing. The smell makes him briefly lightheaded. He looks down at his side, his hands flared with black.

"I can't keep them waiting," she says.

Jason knows he's pushing it. "It's fine."

"Fine—what's fine?"

Hannah strokes Carrie's tawny head as their daughter turns her drawing board right side up to study a recent doodle. The three of them are seated in the living room, which gives the conversation the air of a family meeting.

"Go for it," he says. "I'll cut back. It makes sense."

"So why do you seem down?"

"I'm saying it's fine."

"I don't want it to be *fine*, is the point. I want you to be happy. For me, at least."

It doesn't seem possible for him to be fine, knowing that she's thriving while he isn't. She should be satisfied with him going along with her success.

Carrie turns her head slightly to look at Jason and then back at her drawing board. He'd always expected fatherhood to change him—to unseat his selfishness with renewed purpose.

And it had, certainly, yet it never managed to fully overrule his other selves.

"I know you think this is strictly about my career," Hannah continues, "but it's not. I've thought a ton about what this means for us. Think of a house—you can have a studio space, do whatever the hell you want in it."

He nods. This freedom is not the worst thing to imagine. Perhaps this space would allow for something radical to occur.

"Think of how good it will be for Carrie in the short term. She'll be so happy."

Carrie looks sidelong at Jason before shooting her tongue from her mouth and smiling. "Yeah, Steve, think about me."

Hannah is asleep, pinching the striped comforter between her legs. A gentle wheeze in her nose. Jason looks at her chapped and almost-smiling mouth. He's decided that it's OK to be *fine* with his decision. Hannah had cried after they talked again, after Carrie was down, her tears eased by the gratitude she expressed.

He takes a deep breath. The spray paint is in the hall closet, waiting under the coats and behind the plastic tub with detergents and cleaners. He gets up and walks carefully across the old wood floor. He reaches into the closet and pulls a can free. Next, he eases open the front door and brings his shoes and jacket out into the hallway, resting them on the bench by the mailboxes. The radiator hisses as he pulls his dark beanie from his pocket.

The darkness is muddy outside. The air cool. His shoulders are tight, the spot where his tension is stored. One benefit of cutting back at work is that he will no longer be hunched over for hours every day.

A block away is the renovated movie theater, with its large, exposed wall rising above the roof of its squat neighbor. He crosses the street, walks beneath the deco marquee, wanders down to the alley's entrance. Two cars cruise by, smoke blowing from the passenger window of one.

He's studied the various points of entry and exit while out with Carrie. He must pull himself up onto a low window and from there climb the fire escape. The ladder is flaking, and he regrets not bringing gloves, but without much trouble he makes his way up the metal stairs to the roof's ledge. The view of the street makes him feel unsteady, so he shuts his eyes. The wind whips against his lids.

A dim light is on in Tony's apartment, a floor above his own. Jason wishes he could send him some kind of signal. He wishes Tony could be his witness. He steps over the lip of the roof and then onto a dark swath of something, a loose panel among many scattered across the ground. The surface is softer beneath his feet than he'd imagined.

Jason grabs the can from his coat and takes a wide step back to test the spray against the ground. He trips, his foot catching on the edge of one of the panels. He hits the ground hard. The noise of the can against the roof seems conspicuously loud, and he remains flat on his back to stay out of sight. He feels a sharp pain in his elbow, some nerve-induced static along his forearm. After a minute, he rolls over and crawls to grab the can, resting his hands on it and then laying his head on his hands. There's not much ambient noise except the wind. He looks down at the street, the sidewalks. No movement besides the shimmering trees. He waits for the traffic lights to turn green and gets up to face the wall, spraying with speed. Then he jogs back to the fire escape.

"Steve," her little voice says, "look."

Carrie has gotten free from her pants for a third time and Jason is verging on surrender. It's early all over again. As he remembers the reason why he'd not slept, he's distracted momentarily from his fatigue. "Come on, we're gonna be late."

Carrie is silent at first. "*Foyne*," she says.

Jason is surprised to hear movement in the bedroom. "Come on, Carrie. Let's move it."

Carrie's dress is tucked into the back of her pants, and her feet are bare. He grabs a pair of socks from her closet and sticks them in his pocket, slipping her backpack from the hook beside the kitchen door. His hand is speckled with black.

The bedroom door opens. "Come here for a sec?" Hannah says, through slitted, lizard eyes.

He passes Carrie her balled socks with his clean hand, aware he will have to adjust her socks later.

"Where did you go last night? I came out and you weren't on the couch."

"I was probably in the bathroom?" He turns to Carrie. "You good with your socks, bud?"

"When you were back in bed you smelled . . . smelled like, I don't even know. Like paint."

Jason's hand is hidden by Carrie's sky-blue backpack at his side. "Paint?" he says. "What do you mean?"

Carrie clues in. "I want to paint!"

Hannah furrows her brow. "Is this about my job?"

"You think I'm huffing fumes or something? I don't get it."

She watches him. "Radical honesty, remember?"

"I remember," he says. His chest tightens. What he remembers most immediately is being robbed at fifteen, a crew of kids stealing his backpack of spray paint and emptying it right in front of him while he watched. He'd chosen to do then what he always does: act like he doesn't care. "I went outside. To get fresh air. I couldn't sleep."

She eyes him.

"What? It helped," he says.

Carrie walks past. "Bye, Mommy."

Hannah kisses Carrie's hair. Carrie smiles behind her dangling bangs. She turns to Jason. "Whatever's going on—"

"Don't worry," he interrupts. "Grab some sleep." Before leaving, he blows a kiss through his balled fist. A love-dart gun, as he'd originally conceived of it.

Outside, his tag is a stark glyph in the morning light. It doesn't look as impressive as he'd hoped, but it's there. Carrie, on his shoulders, has an ideal view of it. They walk to the corner and Jason lingers, pretends to search for something inside his jacket. His elbow is sore.

"Go. Go." She bucks on his shoulders. "The light is green."

He stands straight up and positions her toward the theater, but Carrie fails to notice.

At school he kneels to hang the backpack from Carrie's shoulders. She pulls the straps tight as Ms. Adrienne holds the door open.

"You forgot something," he says when Carrie walks in. This is a game they play. She runs back out and hugs him, leans her head on his shoulder.

"Were you all painting?" Ms. Adrienne asks, nodding her curls at his hand.

Tony heads toward Jason on the sidewalk. His van is waiting outside. "Where are you tonight, allegedly, Moat?"

"You and I are grabbing drinks." By sacrificing for Hannah, Jason thinks, he has earned the right to lie.

In the van, he watches the graffiti pass by from the highway. It appears on distant billboards and shadowed underpasses. All the space seems vast.

"I didn't think you'd agree," Tony says.

Jason doesn't read too much into the comment. He repositions his backpack at his feet.

"I got a taste. No turning back."

They exit down a ramp into industrial territory. Tony ducks his head over the steering wheel and looks up through the windshield. He searches the tops of the buildings.

Jason feels nervous suddenly.

"Almost there," Tony says.

They turn onto a long street of warehouses; a broken traffic light down the block flickers. Jason thinks of Hannah sleeping, of Carrie, but shakes himself free of it.

"You're quiet," Tony says.

"Mental preparation," he tries to joke.

Tony parks; the van sighs to silence. The glow from the streetlamps looks toxic.

"It's up there." Tony points to a tall concrete façade.

Jason looks up.

"The water tower is on top."

Jason can't fully see it.

"There's some scaffolding. It blocks the view partially from the highway. Once the construction is complete, all the cars will see."

It feels real now, all of it. Jason pulls his backpack onto his lap. They both scan the surroundings before Tony points to the stepladder in the back seat. "When you're up there make sure the ladder is sturdy before you climb."

He grabs a pair of gloves and hands them to Jason. Then he stops suddenly. Jason stops too. They both listen to the faint sound of sirens.

Tony eyes Jason, grabbing the keys in the ignition, but doesn't turn them. The noise grows jarringly loud before coming to a halt. Tony pulls his hand away and sits back. Lights flare faintly from the adjoining street.

He starts the van then and does a slow 180. At the corner, he makes a right turn and then another, driving past the street where police cars, two of them, have pulled up to a garage. Jason can make out only one officer, leaning against his door.

"What should we do?" Jason asks quietly.

"Do?" Tony fishes his vape from the cup holder. "Go home."

"The cops won't be out there all night."

Tony looks at him with mild surprise. "There will be other nights."

"Can't we drive around, or go grab food and come back? What are the chances they return to this exact spot?"

"The police aren't lightning. It's possible. You know I can't afford to be stopped."

"Think about it, it's probably safer for us that this happened," Jason said.

"There could be more surveillance, backup. Who knows what the fuck goes on inside of that garage?"

Whatever it was fails to compete with Jason's adrenaline. To delay the momentum would be to threaten it completely. He leans back against the headrest.

"Dada Jason." Tony reaches over and squeezes Jason's shoulder. Jason flinches from the surprise, the pain, and shrinks away. "It doesn't have to be right now."

Jason shuts his eyes and grinds his teeth. He rests his hand on the door's handle.

"You'll have your chance."

"Just let me out," he says. "Up here."

"What? No, man. No way."

"Just do it."

Tony stares at him, as if awaiting a punch line. "You're coming home with me."

Jason is silent.

"Don't be crazy."

At the stop sign, Jason grabs his bag and hops out of the passenger seat. Slams the door. Tony rolls down the window and yells after him, but Jason doesn't look back. He jogs down the street, listens for the van to pull away, which eventually it does.

He's cold now, unsure of where he's heading. He pulls on the straps of his backpack. The exercise, should he decide to walk the three or maybe four miles home, will be useful. In the distance, a dark eighteen-wheeler passes by and gradually disappears on the elevated expressway. He flips on his hood, cinches it tight. The backpack bounces gently as he walks, and he can hear, just barely, the sound of cans rattling inside of it.

He waits several minutes before entering an alley halfway down the block. The street is empty. Jason puts his hands in his pockets. A coin from Carrie's toy cash register is mixed in with his spray paint caps, almost the exact shape and weight. He thinks of blowing a raspberry on her taut naked belly.

He pulls a can from his backpack and crouches low, spraying the wall. The fumes are strong, but he continues, standing to spray the crispest version of *Moat* yet.

Back on the street he notices a dumpster. He sprays a large tag on the side of it, but it doesn't show up well against the dumpster's dark green color. He needs to switch to white paint.

A few blocks ahead, Jason notices a van slowly coming toward him. His heart seizes, as he thinks it's the police, but then he notices Tony's face above the steering wheel.

After pulling up, Tony rolls the passenger-side window down. "I couldn't leave you."

"I'm good," he says. "I swear."

Tony turns his head as if alert to something. It sounds to Jason like a car nearby.

"Get in," Tony says.

"Trust me, I'm fine."

Tony responds with a glare. Jason grabs his bag. "Fine, but let's try to find one more spot to hit before we go home."

As they pull off, a car turns the corner behind them. Before Jason registers its blue stripe, he hears a *whoop*. The sound is so startling and loud that it feels as if it strikes him physically.

Tony slows as the lights flash behind them. He grips the wheel with both hands. "Fuck," he mutters, hanging his head.

Jason's heart has set off and won't stop. He rolls his foot along one of the cans inside his backpack on the floor. He thinks of Hannah sleeping, of her waking up with Carrie if he doesn't make it home. Tony is stock-still beside him. Against the nearest wall, outside Jason's window, the red and blue lights steadily dust the brick.

What happens next seems like it has already happened, or like it's choreographed. They exit the van at the officer's instruction. As they're being cuffed, Jason's fingers graze the edge of his key chain, jutting slightly from his back pocket.

HIDE-AND-SEEK

Bruce was finishing a bowl of lukewarm Thai noodles when the door to his hotel room opened. A hazy pane of light spread along the wall.

"Hello?"

A woman peeked into the room's entryway.

"This is the second night I've walked by and noticed your door ajar. You're begging for trespassers."

He recognized the woman now by her cropped copper hair. She held a small backpack and wore flip-flops. He'd seen her one morning at the front desk.

"Hey, sorry," Bruce said, feeling like he'd broken a rule. He grabbed his sweats and stood up. The space was filthy, jeans strewn on the floor and the trash can overflowing with plastic take-out tubs. "I'm afraid that if I shut the door all the way, I'll lock myself out."

She stared back at him blankly.

"I used to fear trapping my son inside the apartment. Not being able to get to him."

This habit of leaving the door cracked to the lobby always drove his wife, Shannon, crazy. Naturally she too worried about trespassers.

"So why're you here, if you have a family?" she asked.

"Living in disgrace."

They spoke in the room's relative dark. She walked over to the desk, where an empty plastic wrapper sat beside a Diet Coke. "For what?" She pulled out the chair and leaned it up on its back legs as if testing its strength.

"My wife found texts. From a co-worker."

"So you fucked her—or him?"

"No—no. I mean, we flirted. Sexting," he said. "What's your name? And why am I explaining this to you?"

"I'm Charlotte."

"Bruce."

"So you're living here now because of texts?"

The easy answer was yes. Bruce was a thirty-five-year-old father living in a La Quinta because of texts. Texts that had come after he'd supposedly reformed himself, after Shannon had found his Tinder profile. He'd willingly left the house as a result. Shannon agreed that they should take some space while figuring out their relationship.

"Don't tell me you bring your son here," she said.

"He thinks I still live at home." Lucas was five, and he always looked for Bruce first when he woke. Bruce left the hotel before sunrise and let himself into the apartment early every morning so he could be there when Lucas got up.

"Do you work here or what?" Bruce asked.

"No— Well, not really," she said. "It's a long story but I'm around a lot. I gotta run. We'll see each other again." She walked to the door. "Can I close this now?"

"Please," he said.

The next morning, at the bakery, Lucas held half his poppy-seed bagel up near his face. "Why do we always eat breakfast here?" Cream cheese streaked his chin and cheek.

"Because we love it."

Lucas turned to the rack by the register, revealing his wiry cowlick. He wanted chips, but Bruce said they needed to prepare for their adventure—they'd have chips later. Without suitable housing, Bruce resorted to making the city their playground, living room, and kitchen. He had recently started looking for apartments, which was daunting. Fortunately, for now, Lucas enjoyed his office. Even though Bruce was on book leave, they'd hang out there on the weekends, when no one was around. It was fun to pour over the art monographs and tape paper onto the wall to make mini murals.

Outside, Bruce reached in his backpack and pulled out a box of sidewalk chalk, which he'd found earlier on the street. Lucas looked skeptical, but Bruce knew he'd get into it once they made it to the park and got started. Lucas asked to ride on Bruce's shoulders, still. He was light enough that it wasn't taxing, and Bruce loved squeezing his son's little calf muscles. They approached Prospect Park with the Saturday-morning hordes: the farmers market savants and cyclists.

He placed Lucas down beside a large rock near the pond where the dogs swam. With a stick of green chalk, Bruce drew little figures on the craggy surface.

"This can be you and me."

Lucas grabbed the pink chalk and began shading sky.

"The oldest art in the world was drawn in caves," Bruce said. "On rocks like these."

"Where?" Lucas leaned in close to carefully dash the rays of a sun. His hair smelled of the honey shampoo Shannon used. Bruce would need to buy his own soon.

"In France," he said. "Someday we'll go on a trip together."

"A daddy and son trip." Lucas wiped his chalky hands in the dirt beside the rock and showed his palms. Two wet dogs bounded past, flicking water. Bruce led Lucas to the pond's edge, where they squatted on a broad stone. They dipped their hands in. The water was cold. They both wiped their hands dry against his pants.

Inscrutably, the closest corner store's ATM was labeled "Young Dad" on its screen. Bruce had never planned on having a kid until his late thirties—not before finishing his book. For Shannon, ten years older, pregnancy at forty-four was urgent. So, he'd heaved himself on top of her at the ovulation device's instruction. The doctor had unruly eyebrows and commended Bruce's virility.

Each week, Bruce paid their nanny, Ewa, in cash. On Friday evenings, he delivered the money and met Shannon and Lucas near the apartment for pizza. He paid for this too. Another item on the savings-depleting ledger.

"How's the continental breakfast?" Shannon asked. They sat outside on the back patio of the restaurant, awaiting their pies.

Shannon wore a creamsicle-colored canvas jacket and turquoise earrings; she'd always had a lovely sense of form and color. Highlights now dashed her dark hair. She looked thinner.

"The kitchen sucks," he said. "I don't even get coffee most days." His room at La Quinta was on the first floor, which meant he caught all the action in and around the lobby. Had he not already been awake at 4:00 that morning, the argument between two men that eventually led to a body being thrown against his door would have scared him shitless. Thank God the door was closed that time.

"How's the series coming?"

Shannon had been working on a series of small sculptures for the last six months. Though she was a social worker now, she'd gone to art school and maintained an admirable dedication to her passion.

"It's not," she said. "I've been distracted."

Lucas squirmed in his chair and tugged his striped shirt. He dipped a disc of bread into his water glass. Bruce felt his son was almost too old for games at the table. Whenever he found a new apartment, Lucas would eat with him like an adult.

Shannon chewed, neatly, and doused her plate in olive oil. "I don't want to make things awkward." She paused to pet Lucas's hair. "I'm seeing someone."

"We see people all the time, Mama." Lucas spoke through his bread-filled mouth.

Bruce's nose twitched. She was looking for a reaction. He turned away, imagining that the strangers surrounding them on the patio assumed they were an intact family. "Makes sense, I guess," he said.

"How long do you plan to remain at your current residence?"

She spoke evasively around Lucas, which seemed to lessen the severity of what they discussed.

"Not sure," he said. "I'm checking out another place next week."

He needed a two-bedroom for Lucas. The options, thus far, had been bleak.

"Well, do you at least have some sort of plan?"

"I don't fucking know." He raised his voice and then lowered it.

Lucas said "*Awwww*."

"I don't know," Bruce whispered.

Lucas looked down then. "Guys—no fighting," he said. "Please."

Shannon sipped her wine and looked away. "Why do I have to act so you don't have to? If you're going to exile yourself, at least have the balls to say what you feel."

He'd never fully articulate what he felt, which he believed had more to do with the feelings' complexity than with his deep fear that the feelings were actually simple.

Shannon's large eyes were glossy. "You're the one who cheated."

"It's not that simple," he said.

"You don't get to define my pain. If you're really ending this, then just say it. Stop dragging it out." She moved her chair back and got up. "Don't force me to act on our behalf. Your inaction is oppressive. Coward."

"You're right," he said. "I'm sorry." He reached for her, but Shannon dodged his hand. She leaned over to kiss Lucas's head.

"Let's go," she said. "You want ice cream, honey?"

Lucas raised alternating arms in excitement.

Bruce saw the waiter and signaled for the bill.

"Daddy, what flavor are you getting?"

"Aw, bud," Bruce said. "I've got to go to the office. I'm sorry."

"Now?" Lucas asked.

Shannon spoke then. "Daddy's got a lot of important things to figure out," she said. "At least he won't be there to take big bites from our cones."

The following weekend, Bruce picked Lucas up after breakfast and they headed for his office. He'd left some research materials there.

Bruce's book was tentatively titled *Art Public*, and he wasn't sure he even believed in the premise anymore. Maybe being adrift had drained his enthusiasm for writing. It was merciful that he wouldn't have to churn out another thousand words on some spiritless exhibition for the magazine for a while, even if he wasn't spending his leave wisely. Bruce needed to finish a draft of the manuscript to get paid.

In a bus shelter near the subway, he noticed an ad for an Irving Penn show at the Met. He hadn't gone to the Met in ages. He'd first taken Lucas when he was six weeks old.

"Daddy, you're the weirdest person I know." Lucas spoke through a smile from high on Bruce's shoulders. He bent over to whisper in Bruce's ear, repeating himself.

"No actually, *you're* the weirdest, not me."

"Nope," Lucas said.

The joke continued until they reached the subway. Bruce felt for his wallet, patting the front pocket of his pants, but it wasn't there.

"What happened?" Lucas asked.

"We have to make a pit stop," Bruce said. His other, dirtier pants were hanging on the back of the chair in his room.

"What's a pit stop?"

"It's a term from racing," Bruce said. "It'll be quick."

They walked a few avenues west, hard shadows stenciled on the sidewalk. Bruce had never looked up at the façade of the the La Quinta in the morning. It almost didn't look foreboding.

Charlotte stood outside, at the top of the steps. She wore a sweatshirt with the arms cut off, holding a phone at her ear. She came down and removed her oversize sunglasses before looking at Lucas.

She hung up the phone. "I'm Charlotte." Smiling, she reached out a hand.

Lucas leaned over onto Bruce's head and hid his face.

Bruce hoisted Lucas off his shoulders. "Charlotte is my colleague," he said. "She helps me with research." He widened his eyes at her.

Lucas waved shyly and then gave Charlotte a high five as she offered her flattened palm.

"Will you stay with Charlotte for a sec, bud? I just need to run to the bathroom."

Lucas wrapped his arms around Bruce's leg.

"Do you like Snickers?" Charlotte asked.

“Yeah,” Lucas said. His eyes brightened.

“Follow me,” she said.

Lucas took her hand, and she walked him toward the small kitchen area as Bruce went to get his wallet. When he was back, Lucas already had chocolate beneath his nose.

“None for me?” Bruce asked.

Lucas shook his head.

“So what’s today’s adventure?” Charlotte asked.

“The office,” Lucas said plainly.

“Hey, we’re gonna have fun, bud!”

“When I was young, my dad used to take me to the Met,” Charlotte said. “He’d set up scavenger hunts and draw little miniatures of the works, like a key. I’d fold them up in my pocket and we’d walk around until I found them all. It took hours. It was our favorite thing to do.”

“Can we do that instead, Daddy?” Lucas asked. “Please?”

“Another time, I promise.” He eyed Charlotte. “Your dad still out there making all of us look bad?”

“He passed away a few years ago.”

“I’m sorry,” Bruce said.

Lucas opened his second mini-Snickers. He didn’t seem to be paying attention to them.

“I live with my mom in Astoria, in my childhood home. He was an artist, with a ton of debt. When the bills show up, my mom curses his name like he’s still in the next room. The idiot thought he would figure it all out in time.”

Bruce tried to picture the man. “Why are you at a La Quinta in Brooklyn if you live in Astoria?”

"I went to high school with a guy who franchised this one. He lets me have unused rooms for cheap. I have an OnlyFans," she said.

Bruce perked up.

"I used to try and record in my room at home, but I couldn't handle the guilt. The money is crazy, though, so I can't afford to stop. I'll have my mom's second mortgage paid down by the end of the year."

Income as intriguing as it was inconceivable to Bruce. "Is there an appetite for the opinions of midtier art critics?"

"There's an appetite for everything," she said.

Later that night, Bruce lay with his notebook straddling his stomach. His pen rested on his thigh. The imperative for money was supposed to help him generate words, but instead he pictured Charlotte, somewhere in a room above him, fingering herself on camera. Once, he'd walked in on Shannon using her vibrator. After his initial surprise, a relief set in to know that she was actually getting off.

He stared at the wall beside the bed. He'd taped up a painting Lucas had done at his office—thick black lines and broad fields of bright color. The image was more compelling than anything he could hope to write. The small brushstrokes were so instinctual and unburdened by intention.

His phone lit up on the bed. It was nearly midnight, and the screen displayed a series of messages from Shannon. She was worried about a growth, or lump, she said. She had a history of cysts and fibroids, which had made pregnancy hard. She was scared and wanted him to come over and look.

He left the hotel quickly. When he arrived at Shannon's, she led him into the dimly lit kitchen. Lucas's bedroom door was cracked and his white noise machine whirred.

"Give me your hand," Shannon whispered. She slipped the waist of her pajama pants down.

He closed his eyes as she pressed his fingers into her labia. Her breath fell gently on him.

"I'm not crazy, right?" she asked. "It's there."

"You're not crazy." Bruce looked out from the kitchen into the living room. He'd have to come get all his books if he moved. He realized how different the living room would be without the filled shelves. Lucas would wake up to the emptiness of an exposed wall.

"I'm sorry," Shannon said. "I started to get paranoid that I was imagining it. I don't trust myself sometimes." She flipped her hair to one side and let it lie on her shoulder.

Bruce went to the sink and rinsed his fingers under warm water.

"You can stay if you want." She spoke sweetly. "Sleep on the couch, whatever."

Bruce looked at her legs, her thighs in spandex. The thought of sharing a bed with her again made him tense. He refused to face the expectation in her eyes. "I've hardly been sleeping as it is," he said. "I really need to get some writing done."

Shannon nodded vaguely and walked back into her room as he slipped his shoes on. He looked toward the gap of darkness at Lucas's door. One day, much later in life, he wanted to tell

Lucas about this exact moment. He would tell him that he was a flawed man, that he'd thought his indiscretions were anomalous until they revealed a pattern, and then he didn't stop. He would tell Lucas that all of this was about figuring out how to be his authentic self in order to be a good father.

The following week, the ATM made Bruce consider the crisis of the arts. Charlotte had suggested they go to the Met together (she loved Irving Penn), and even though Bruce had a membership for work, he always donated because museums, like him, were hard up.

When he arrived, the sun hadn't quite broken free of the building tops. Charlotte was seated on the grand steps, her legs covered in gooseflesh.

"First time seeing art with a real critic," she said.

"You're the fan, I'm not sure how much I'll have to add."

The line to enter was long but moving. Charlotte checked her phone several times and Bruce wondered if it was OnlyFans related. He suddenly felt foolish and wanted to retreat to the hotel. He missed Lucas.

Inside the grand atrium, patrons walked with hands clasped behind their backs. Bruce grazed Charlotte's arm as they entered, which was the first time they'd touched. She led him toward several large photographs of bodies in the initial room. She paused at a picture of an androgynous figure bent forward, almost praying. She studied it.

"One of my favorites." She leaned even closer. "The spine is like a skipping stone."

Her metaphor loosened the image. Bruce thought the connection was lovely.

"Apparently he put bleach in the developer, to get the texture," she said.

"I should try cutting my coffee with some," Bruce said.

She smirked without laughing. "Don't fetishize your pain."

At each print, she lingered. Bruce had always been accused of moving too quickly through exhibitions, even by Shannon. He'd always felt that spending the same length of time at each work, being deliberate in that way, was the kind of movement that art should resist. The urge should be spontaneous, free.

In the next, larger room, enormous prints of the human form covered the walls. Charlotte strode over to a woman's midsection. *Nude No. 72*. Bruce stood beside her and looked at the shadows across the skin. A prominent mole looked like the eye of a face whose smile was a fold in her stomach.

"To me, this is what we see when we fuck."

She pronounced the curse like it might scandalize him.

"The awkwardness is sensual," she continued. "These are moments of pure body."

Her words seemed almost performative, yet he was envious of how closely they might approximate her feelings.

"I think Penn treats nudity with dignity. Letting yourself go is integral to sexuality. Nothing is sexier than someone reveling in themselves, giving themselves over without hesitation."

"With Shannon," he started. He rarely talked to others about his sex life. "I spent a lot of time trying to justify our sexless life." Seeking a sexual outlet elsewhere seemed easier than breaking through with Shannon. "The truth is always simpler."

"Occam's razor," Charlotte said. "You just have to let it cut you a little."

The final room had Penn's portraits. Bruce was drawn, as he'd always been, to the picture of Saul Steinberg in a suit with a paper bag over his head. His nose poked out through a slit and his eyes were hidden behind two ragged holes.

"I could've guessed." Charlotte sidled up to him. No one else was close. "Isn't it exhausting to keep running from yourself?"

He felt both gall and admiration.

"I traffic in depravity and repression," she said. "So much of it is pretending. I know an Artful Dodger when I see one." She watched Bruce. Her eyes squinted quickly as if she hadn't spoken. The additional beat of attention gave him pause.

After the final room, Bruce was expecting to check out another show or two before they left. Charlotte had to cut their time short to help her mom sort through their basement storage. Bruce wasn't sure what to do with the rest of his afternoon.

As they exited the museum together, a woman tossed breadcrumbs to a group of frantic pigeons at her feet.

"You haven't even told me what you actually do *only* for your fans," he said.

"I stick my finger in the holes." She darted a V shape at Bruce with her fingers. She stared. "I tear off the mask."

"And this gets you off?"

"It gets *them* off."

"And you?"

"For me it's work, but work I enjoy. There's an uncomplicated pleasure in giving someone what they want."

He lingered on the word *want*. Were he one of her paying customers, what would he even ask for? "So how can I see?"

She rubbed her fingers together, signaling money.

He chuckled. "I'm short on disposable income. Unless your boy can get me a discount on a La Quinta suite like yours."

"We can figure out an arrangement," she said. "I have thoughts."

He couldn't tell what she meant, but he was eager to find out.

"We'll talk about it later," she said. "I'll be back in Brooklyn tonight."

That night, at the hotel, he didn't even try to write. He checked his phone every few minutes to see if Charlotte had texted. On other nights, when he couldn't sleep, he started walking along Third Avenue, enjoying the night's anonymity. This act, only a month before, would have seemed insane. He left his room and walked past the lobby, where a TV played a movie with Jamie Foxx. He found the stash of candy in the kitchen and ate several mini 3 Musketeers, which he didn't even like, as a distraction.

When he got back to his room, Charlotte finally texted: *Come to 5L.* He'd never been above the second floor. He suddenly felt that there was so much to do before meeting her; he had no idea what to expect. He was out of toothpaste so brushed with the remaining bit of mouthwash he had.

When he got upstairs, door 5L was cracked. He pushed it open carefully and peeked: quiet and mostly dark. It seemed like a trick at first. A desk chair had been positioned in front of the bed. Charlotte came out from the bathroom with her finger at her lips. Held it there. She wore a skintight suit so threadbare it revealed her entire body underneath, like a kind of net. She eyed him and then the bed, back and forth, still without speaking. Bruce saw the laptop pitched open; it had been hard to notice in the dark. A tall ring light stood unplugged in the corner. Charlotte walked over to the computer. Its screen showed the chair, and she started pacing back and forth in front of it. Her likeness was delayed slightly on the screen, her skin blurring. This was being livestreamed, he realized. Bruce held his entire body still. It was like he was trapped, though he remained off-screen. Theatrically, Charlotte grabbed something with the two forefingers she had been resting on the chair. She held Bruce's hand and led him into the frame. She looked at him for a few seconds, inspecting him as if she was deciding something, but as she turned away, her body blocked him from the screen. Then she reached both arms behind his head and pulled something over his face. He winced as a softness covered his cheeks. He prepared to struggle for breath, but his lips tasted free air through a hole. His eyes blinked through dark halos: a balaclava.

Gently, she sat him down in the chair. Her every move was unhurried, which had a calming effect. After her hands grazed him, she judiciously unbuttoned and loosened his clothes. Not one article at a time, but a portion of each, revealing him bit by bit. Bruce began to get hard as she reached for his pants. She tugged slowly at his zipper and then ran warm palms up and down his thighs. The screen showed him—them—and he watched himself. He was the subject, but also the viewer, one among many, he assumed. He wasn't sure where to look but was calmed by his anonymity. He focused on the shadow of a seam bubbling in the wallpaper above the bed, coming undone.

Charlotte pulled his hands back behind the chair, and he felt inflexible. She fastened them together with something he couldn't see, coarse like twine. He was naked now save for his socks, grateful he'd showered earlier. His body felt cold. He locked his jaw to prevent shivering. His erection was center screen. He flexed and it bobbed as Charlotte crept around him. Bruce felt a deep urge and jerked forward, almost forgetting he was bound. She bent down between his legs and put her hands on his thighs. His body warmed. When she stared at him, he momentarily forgot the screen, himself. He desired her to an excruciating degree; the constraint only fed the feeling. She ran a lip just barely along his dick and pulled away. Bruce wondered if she could feel his heart pumping. The way it seemed to fuel his entire body.

She rose, tracing a finger across his chest. Then suddenly she grabbed the back of his neck. She turned around and lowered herself slowly on top of him, dominating the screen. Facing it. Charlotte's back was a field of pale diamonds. Her heat on him, everywhere. His dick was like the beginning of a taut, finely woven cord running through him. When she got up it was as if everything had been pulled away, deadened. Bruce dove forward at her small, plump butt. This was a partial performance, and it was only him on-screen now. As he sat in the quiet, his pulse came into focus. He felt helpless. He suddenly imagined Shannon, at home on the couch, watching him. The dueling glare of the monitors.

The light from the bathroom came on. The brightness was distracting. Charlotte walked out a moment later in a gray tank top and sweats.

She clapped the laptop closed and sat on the edge of the bed beside it. "Not bad, Artful Dodger."

Her smile cut hard against the moment. Bruce tried to pull his hands apart, which burned his skin. "What's wrong with you?"

She looked down at his dick then. Not being able to cover it was brutal. Whatever spirit had taken hold of Bruce quickly vanished.

"You seemed into it." She grabbed a small pair of scissors from the bathroom and snipped him free.

His arousal had been replaced by something leaden. He grabbed his pants and pulled them up. His chest was bare and chilly. He felt used. "That was some sick idea," he said. He started to laugh then, hysterically, from the surplus of unspent energy.

"You'll thank me in a second," she said.

She grabbed her phone from the table. "You have Venmo?"

He nodded, and she took his phone in her other hand and photographed the QR code on her screen. "Keep our transactions private."

He read the numbers several times, attempting to correct the order of the digits.

"That's just for this time," she said. "We'll make more now that they've seen it. We had chemistry, man."

"I can't take five thousand dollars from you."

"That's Venmo's daily limit. This is only half."

Which was more inconceivable, the speed with which he'd gotten the money or the act of earning it? The details were intangible and seemed fake.

"When things get extreme, I throw out extreme numbers to make it worthwhile. This group of guys was begging. They wanted to see you, to imagine being you, a captive."

Bruce was stunned as the information continued to settle. Only the day before, he'd been with his son at the office drawing pictures.

"You'd never have agreed to this had I presented it to you casually," she said. "Nevertheless, you made a choice."

The next weekend Bruce took Lucas to IKEA. Before he'd had a kid, the very notion of visiting IKEA had made a nihilist of him. Now, with Lucas riding around on a shopping cart like a ship, the store was a horizon of possibility.

"Look!" Lucas recognized the mini step stool with a grid of green dots. "That's the same one we have."

Bruce wanted to gauge what things Lucas might like for a future bedroom without him knowing about it yet. Bruce had found an apartment and was able to act on it quickly with the extra cash, which was only the beginning of a new income stream, if Charlotte was to be believed.

"We definitely need this," Lucas said. He ran over to a small tent with a tunnel connected to it. "Can we get it? Please?"

"Not today, bud. We're just browsing."

Bruce knew it was risky, bringing Lucas here, because he hadn't told Shannon about the lease. But in his mind, getting an apartment was the beginning of any possible reconciliation with her.

Lucas looked disappointed. Bruce turned to survey the space. "I've got an idea."

"What?"

"Let's play hide-and-seek."

"OK, but you're counting first," Lucas said.

Bruce thought about Charlotte as soon as he covered his face to count. He hadn't gotten such vigorous, spontaneous erections since high school. But he felt like an idiot for asking her to grab dinner. She'd said she couldn't, without any explanation, and then disappeared for several days. Finally, she'd texted him back, ominously, that she wanted to talk.

He shook himself loose from the fantasy. He crept toward the tent Lucas had wanted earlier. He jumped up and peered through the top, but Lucas wasn't inside. He got low and scoured the cushions and tables. Another little boy ran past, and Bruce reached out before realizing it wasn't Lucas. Slowly, he scanned the tabletops and chairs. Lucas was nowhere. At the opposite end of the kids' area, Bruce didn't spot him and tried to remain calm. "Lucas," he called. "Lucas!" People began noticing. Bruce brushed against the flow of bodies. He stood on his tiptoes and ducked low. In the next space, with kitchen cabinets and countertops, he moved through a maze of surfaces. Finding nothing, Bruce retraced his steps; he ended up in the mobbed café. His stomach tightened. "Lucas!" he called again. He walked quickly back out to the kids' area and over to the tent. Still empty.

A tall man with a dark buzz cut grabbed his forearm. His hands were large, and he held one of the blue IKEA bags. "He's OK," the man said. "Over here."

Bruce rushed around the corner to the living room furniture. Lucas sat on a pale yellow sofa with tears running down his face. He looked like he was trying hard to conceal his sadness, squeezing his hands in his lap. Bruce had never noticed him do this before.

Lucas sat straight up when he saw Bruce; Bruce fell to his knees. Lucas grabbed his neck and wrapped his legs around his father's back. Bruce struggled to stand. The tall man looked at him, not quite gravely, before wandering off.

"You're the best hide-and-seek player in history," Bruce said in Lucas's ear. Lucas didn't respond, but the relief to be holding him was immense. "Are you OK?"

"Yeah," Lucas said. He wiped his cheek with a forearm.

"I bet that was scary," Bruce said.

"Why did you leave?"

"I didn't, bud. I was counting."

"It was taking forever." Lucas sniffled.

"Let's go to the toy bins," Bruce said. "I'll let you pick something out."

"I thought you said we couldn't get anything."

"I changed my mind," Bruce said.

The bar Charlotte asked to meet at was close to the La Quinta; Bruce had passed it on his late-night walks. Besides them, only two older men drank together; one of them was the owner tending bar.

Charlotte looked even more beautiful, her hair a little straggly and flipped to one side. Bruce's urge to fuck her had only grown since she'd declined his invitation to dinner.

"I don't want to make it weird, and this isn't the reason why I asked to chat," she began. "But I'm not going to sleep with you—not off camera, anyway."

Bruce sipped from the tight ring of his High Life bottle.

"I know this can get confusing, but I just want to be up-front about it."

Bruce started sinking into himself, then bolted upright to combat the feeling. Charlotte had been something of a revelation to him, a symbol of thrilling possibility. "OK," he started. "That's fine."

"Dooooon't," she said. "If you were unattractive, I wouldn't ask you to make content with me. It's just much cleaner if we're going to work together."

"I get it."

"One of the guys who follows me on OF lives around here," she said. "He's the dad of a young kid."

Bruce flipped through his Rolodex of dads and tried to imagine them jerking off to him. Or watching him jerk off. "So what does that mean?"

"Nothing, really. It's just that usually there's a critical distance between me and viewers, but sometimes shit like this happens. It's not a big deal, I just wanted to be transparent."

"I'm not worried." He told himself the risk was minimal, the reward crucial. "It's not like I'm going to do it forever."

Charlotte swigged the last of her whiskey. "That's what they all say." A small ice cube slid along the bottom of the glass. "I have a scenario in mind for another video," she said. "It involves you masturbating."

"OK," he said. "Alone, or . . . ?"

"I'll still be in control, but there's a serious edging component."

"Am I still wearing a mask?"

She nodded.

"Why won't you tell me more?"

"There has to be an element of surprise, so your reaction feels natural. Verisimilitude. That's what made the last one so great."

On their next Saturday together, Lucas balanced on a low stone perimeter wall at Prospect Park.

"Remember Travis?"

Travis was their shared conjuring, a gentle, misunderstood monster with green fur and three eyes who lived in the woods.

"I bet you he's out there, alone in the forest, making some tea," Bruce said.

Lucas hopped down, and they walked along a narrow path. He found a tree stump to climb. "Do people draw on trees, like those caves you were talking about?" He stood at the stump's center as if it were a stage.

"People carve things into trees."

"Carve?" Lucas asked.

"Like when you take a knife and cut into something." Bruce kneeled to look at the pale wood of the stump. He rubbed his palm across the flat plane of concentric rings. "Remember the cradle Grandma gave you?"

Lucas nodded.

"That's carved."

"It's not broken anymore," Lucas said.

"Really?" Bruce had forgotten about its loose leg.

"Phil fixed it."

"Phil? Who's Phil?"

"Mommy's friend."

"You saw Mommy's friend fix it? When?"

"A while ago, in the morning."

Lucas's temporal sense was unstable. *A while ago* might've been a week. Or yesterday. Bruce stood up and pulled out his phone. He texted harried lines to Shannon.

"I want to see Travis," Lucas said. He set off ahead on the path, impatient.

Bruce stared at the screen. A moment later Shannon replied: *We'll talk about it later.*

That night, at Shannon's, Lucas was sleeping in his room as Bruce lay on the couch. He was waiting for Shannon to return from her night out, which he hated doing but for the bedtime routine with Lucas. Tonight was markedly worse. His eyes darted around the living room, pausing on the new rug with a geometric pattern that Shannon had bought. He pictured another man sitting at its center, playing with Lucas.

The keys jangled for several seconds before the front door opened. Shannon paused to toe her shoes off in the walkway, leaning a hand on the wall. She didn't look up as she went into the kitchen to place her bag on the counter.

He stood and approached her. She smirked and her eyes were heavy. She was clearly tipsy.

"Did you have this guy in the house with Lucas?" he asked.

"Yeah—so what?" She didn't even hesitate.

"What were you thinking?"

"It's not a big deal."

"Not a big deal?" His heart thumped. "You let a stranger into the house, and he spent the night in the room next to our son?" He stepped closer and clenched his teeth.

"Oh." Her eyes slowly drifted from his. "Now you care? You barely reacted when I told you."

"This isn't about me."

"You want to talk about risk—I know you lost Lucas," she said, "at IKEA. He told me how scared he was. Why did you even take him there?"

"Something to do," he said. "Besides, we were playing hide-and-seek!"

She eyed him. "You got an apartment, didn't you?"

Bruce knew lying was impossible. "I did."

"Jesus, Bruce, why do I always have to mine this information out of you?" She turned to hide her face.

"I didn't say anything to Lucas about the apartment. I wanted the three of us to talk. I was waiting for the right moment."

Shannon went into her room and shut the door. Bruce stood for a moment, listening to the white noise coming through Lucas's cracked door. When he came into the bedroom, he noticed, on the headboard, the small vase Shannon had made for him last year, which he'd used for change.

Shannon was lying on the bed. "Why are you here?"

"Let me stay," he said.

"Fuck you, Bruce." She spoke without much force, which gave her words new weight. "I don't want you here."

"Shannon, I'm sorry," he said. "I want to stay." Bruce wiped his eyes though he wasn't yet crying. He hated seeing her like this, her face buried in a pillow.

She said something, but her words were muffled. She lifted her head. "What are you sorry for?"

"Please, just let me stay," he said. "We can talk in the morning. It's late."

"Tell me."

"I'm sorry that I can't face what I did."

She rose up on an elbow and looked at him. Some of her lipstick had smudged at the corner of her lip, and it almost looked like she'd eaten a Popsicle. "Can't or won't?" she asked.

"I wanted to be desired more than I wanted you."

"Get out," she yelled then. "Get out!"

Bruce listened for Lucas, worried that he might wake up. On the bed beside Shannon, her phone lit up with a text from Phil. She didn't notice, nor did she move. Her eyes were shut. Bruce wanted to grab the phone, but he wasn't even sure why. As he left the room, he shut the door firmly behind him.

After three weeks, Bruce's apartment was still barren, though its ornate detail and gaudy chandeliers made it marginally less depressing in the dark. He had only an air mattress, with an ill-fitting sheet that never stayed in place, and the IKEA tent, still wrapped, in the corner of his room.

He stared at the small bottle of Ro Sparks ED pills, which he'd gotten after several failures to get hard while filming. He'd let his beard grow out, and the balaclava he wore was less of a novelty, making his jaw itch whenever they shot. Once he'd had to stop jerking off and rip the mask off just to breathe the free air.

CABIN PRESSURE

Cam noticed a woman in the security line at JFK, a young mom with a pierced septum and a backpack that mirrored, just, the small child stowed in a carrier on her chest. A tattoo peeked from the woman's collar. Cam thought of childhood, how he'd told his dad he was destined to be a cool parent because he planned to get at least several tattoos. His dad would scoff and roll his eyes; being cool was beside the point, and parenting would be much harder than he could imagine. Cam had gotten a single tattoo, tucked into the fold of his inner forearm. He rubbed it now, as he waited in line. He rarely wore T-shirts, even in the summer, preferring to roll up his sleeve to keep it covered.

"Gate's this way," Nancy said.

Cam turned. He hadn't flown with his younger sister since they were kids. She was twenty-eight now—established in New York—and had hosted him in her one-bedroom in the East Village. She was sweet to accompany him back home to his wife and son.

Near the gate, he wanted another coffee. "You want one?"

"I don't know how you function on so much caffeine," she said.

Cam survived on coffee until dinner, which was typically his only meal of the day. His hunger had lost its vitality, and he'd shed twenty pounds in the last year. Swearing off alcohol helped too, though he'd struggled not to order a drink alone on the flight out.

He grabbed his bag. He and Nancy approached the stanchions. The woman from the security line, with her child, walked by carrying a bag of fast food. She set her backpack down at the end of a row of seats and pulled out a sandwich, taking a bite inches from her baby's head. She bounced as she ate. Cam rubbed his tattoo. He remembered how his hips would ache from bouncing his daughter, Jackie, and how, even when he was alone, it had become instinctual, reflexive. The way her weight had stayed with him. He'd bounce while waiting for the bus or in line to order food. His wife used to laugh at this.

On the plane, he found their row and stashed his duffel beneath the seat in front of him. He hadn't noticed, before, that a part of his canvas belt was snagged in the zipper.

"You gonna help me or what, big bro?" his sister asked.

"Sorry," he said. He stood and hoisted up his sister's suitcase, stowing it in the overhead.

They sat, and Nancy checked her fantasy results on her phone. She'd been a D1 basketball player at UConn and the sole athletic member of their family. Andrew, Cam's son, texted her about basketball constantly and was so excited whenever she flew out to watch him play.

At his feet, Cam looked at the belt in his bag. It was too big for him, even with the three additional holes he'd poked out, but he kept it with him anyway. One tiny sticker had remained stuck:

a glittering magenta smiley face with a rainbow's worth of other colors that his daughter had placed on. Jackie used to love pulling up his shirt to see how many there were. Now he rubbed his finger across the smooth sticker. One side was peeling up, and it seemed miraculous that it was still attached. Cam would periodically pick at it, as if it were a scab, as if he were testing its facility for permanence.

A voice startled him. "We're sitting there." The woman with the tattoos pointed at the window seat next to him.

Nancy rose, and Cam zipped the belt away quickly and got up, stepping into the aisle. He offered to lift the woman's bag, for which Nancy gave a secret, silent applause.

The woman thanked him and sat down, her child still strapped in the carrier. Cam wondered if the woman was coming or going, which coastal city she called home. Maybe her husband was in San Francisco waiting, or maybe she'd never been married and had done this all on her own. Either way, she appeared practiced in her care.

Cam tried to settle as she pulled the baby out. He lowered the armrest. Nancy noticed and gripped his forearm for a moment. The little boy wore a pair of patterned overalls and was maybe eighteen months old. The child turned his head. Cam felt his stare and smiled, turning away. He swallowed deeply then, a tension pulling at his stomach.

The window was bright, and Cam eyed it momentarily. The evening light was chalky, like something had been scribbled in the clouds and had left a fine layer of silt on the world below. The woman cooed at the baby, wobbling him on the two unstable planks of her thighs.

"You want some water?" Nancy offered Cam a bottle from her bag.

"I'm fine." He was fidgeting too much, he knew. Nancy had kindly emptied her apartment of alcohol for his visit. She'd gone with him to two meetings. He'd never expected to be reliant on his little sister.

He turned back to the woman and her baby. "What's his name?"

"Lloyd," she said.

"Eighteen months?"

"Close—twenty."

"How's he on flights?"

"I forgot to do the thing where I bring treats as penance for everyone sitting around us. I can give you a bite of my chicken sandwich if he squeals." She smiled. "He's typically OK though."

The woman had a small, round face and dark hair tightly pulled back. She looked even younger to him now, up close. Jackie had been a surprise—an exciting one—born almost fourteen years after Andrew. Years ago, before Andrew was born, Cam had been so anxious at the prospect of having a son, but in the last year Andrew had proven himself perhaps the strongest while facing the family's loss. He was the only one who was brave enough to talk about her.

As the plane took off, Cam pulled the seat belt tight around his waist. He felt the increasing speed in his chest, and his heart rate seemed intent on matching it. He braced, breathing deeply and carefully.

"Did you check in with Kate?" Nancy asked. "How is she?"

He'd texted with his wife before they'd gotten to the gate. She'd said Andrew had forced them out of the house for a walk.

They'd gone to Dolores Park. Kate had blamed Cam at first, before he'd accepted culpability within himself. They were both to blame, though it was impossible that they shared in the blame evenly. Being in the house together was a constant reminder of this damning fact. Cam had been grateful for a week away.

"I'll stay with you guys for as long as you need me," Nancy said.

"You've done so much for me, sis."

"Really—I have so much PTO."

Lloyd, next to him, began to squirm and whimper. Cam shut his eyes then. Flying had always been easy for him, but now he couldn't think beyond the sheer magnitude of both the vessel and the speed, the dozens of unseen factors one chose to trust in to remain safe and, despite these, how easy it was to conjure an incomprehensible tragedy. The boy cried now. Cam's jaws were clamped. He pushed himself against his seat. He imagined the small smiling sticker on his belt, like a pearl in the muck of his duffel bag.

Once they'd reached their cruising altitude, the woman leaned her seat back and shut her eyes. Lloyd had calmed, handling a ring toy on her lap. Cam had brought the grief memoir Nancy made him promise he'd read, but he'd barely touched it. He couldn't get through more than a few paragraphs of anything, not even *The New York Times*, which he only used to play Spelling Bee, a dependable distraction from the pain.

Cam felt something along his arm and sat up. Gooseflesh broke out on his skin. Lloyd was pulling at his shirt.

"I'm sorry," the woman said. "Stay over here with me, bud," she said to the boy.

Cam smiled and said it was fine. Nancy eyed him. He smiled back at her through tight lips. A moment later Lloyd pulled himself up using a bunch of Cam's shirt. The boy looked unsteady, like he might fall, and Cam's heart skipped. He reached out to catch the child's small arm, and Lloyd giggled, leaning his weight further into Cam. The boy's rib cage was wide and barrel-like—he was much heavier than Cam expected. Cam imagined the weight was difficult for the small woman to lug around, but he thought about the warmth of the boy pressed against her. He hadn't held a young child in some time, and the intimacy of this tiny, hard body was unsettling. Soon Lloyd was fully in Cam's lap. Cam stared at the boy's tall forehead, the fine hairs around his eyebrows, and then the woman grabbed him back onto her lap.

"He's typically not comfortable with strangers," she said. "He's into you."

Lloyd tilted his head back and remained watching Cam. Cam stuck his tongue out and looked away, repeating this until a smile crept onto Lloyd's face. In turn Cam smiled too. Nancy eyed him approvingly. Cam felt a sudden brightness, a sensation he knew was fleeting as soon as it registered. A suffusion of hope. The cruelty lay in its absence, how the shape of something that had once been there remained.

He stood in the aisle after returning from the bathroom. His hips were tight from how clenched he'd kept his body, but now his face was cool from the water he'd splashed on it. He stretched his back and legs. He wished there were other empty seats so he could lay his body out. Then he could sleep through all of this. Nancy had closed her eyes, her mouth barely parted.

The female flight attendant tapped Cam and pointed at the fasten-seat-belt sign. The turbulence that followed shook them. He sat down. He stilled himself in his seat, holding firm as the plane rumbled. Worse than that was the way one of the overhead compartment doors rattled ceaselessly. He imagined it coming undone—unhinged and torn away—the first piece of the plane being stripped clean of its parts by the wind and pressure. No one else on the plane seemed to notice.

The woman beside him stared from her window, peacefully, once the plane settled. Lloyd turned curious again, a sly look of expectation on his chubby face. Cam mustered a half-smile, his energy depleted, a weight having settled on his chest. He had no choice but to sit with it. The weight might continue to grow, taking on so many new leaden bars that the plane wouldn't be able to bear it. He imagined a collision with another plane on a separate course several miles below them; he imagined drowning in some unknown body of water.

Through the window, the woman gazed at the wing slicing the wispy clouds. Lloyd reached for Cam again, pulling at the sleeve rolled up at his elbow. He continued until Cam's tattoo showed. When Lloyd saw the dark numbers on Cam's arm, he fixated. He rubbed his miniature finger across them, the sharp edge of his nail running a slow jagged line on Cam's skin.

The woman noticed again. "Lloyd, buddy, leave the poor man alone," she said.

Cam rolled the sleeve back down to cover his tattoo.

"What're you doing, bud? Huh?" She nuzzled the boy's nose and then turned to Cam. "What's the date?" she asked. "Sorry to be nosy."

Cam didn't think she'd seen the tattoo. Sobriety was the simple answer that foreclosed on too many follow-up questions.

She gave him a solemn look and nodded, congratulated him. "Do you have kids?" she asked. "You're so good with mine."

Cam grabbed his elbow reflexively. He could feel the line Lloyd had drawn with his nail and imagined the fine scab it might leave behind. "Yeah," he said, nodding his head. "My son's sixteen."

Nancy clued in. "He's a great dad. His son's the starting point guard on his high school team."

"Is that basketball? Sorry, I'm dense," the woman said.

Cam nodded. A warmth gathered along his chest, and sweat dotted his sideburns.

"I wonder what sport you'll be into, my little dude," she said to Lloyd.

Cam wondered where along the flight's trajectory they were, and when the exact moment would be that the plane started its slow descent to reach the ground again. He wanted to set his feet down, to feel sturdy. He pulled at the skin around his tattoo. The numbers of the date stretched and settled back into form. That day, a year ago, like any other day. Almost everything about it rote. Temporary tattoos of unicorns and cupcakes and suns were scattered around their apartment—they'd bought too many for Jackie's second birthday party the week before. In the evening, Kate was giving Jackie a bath and her boss called. She stepped away for a minute to take it, calling out to Cam to swap places (Andrew was still at practice). Cam didn't hear her, or he'd tuned it out, that voice constantly asking for something. It was impossible to know now among the many unstable memories of that day. Cam had walked down the hall to the bathroom and seen Jackie's arm hanging out of the tub. He smiled to himself. She'd intentionally wanted to keep it dry to protect the unicorn on her forearm—she'd done so every night since her party. Once Cam fully entered the bathroom, it was too late. He screamed for Kate as he pulled Jackie's slippery body free from the water.

Cam felt a return of the urge. It would rear and subside depending on the day, the hour, the minute. He stared at the illuminated button above his seat, imagining how easy it would be to summon an attendant—God!—pouring a tiny bottle of whiskey over ice, the cold, soothing liquid moving through him. He'd gone through a period of steady drunkenness in the early days of his leave of absence from work, before fully acknowledging his problem.

Lloyd had fallen asleep in the cradle of his mother's arms, and she leaned back in her seat without closing her eyes. Cam realized he didn't even know her name. He didn't want to.

"I never thought I'd have him," she said.

Cam was surprised.

"I didn't picture myself as a mother. It happened out of nowhere, with a guy I'd only been seeing for two months." She petted Lloyd's head gently. "But he saved me."

The thought flashed in Cam's mind, as it often did, ex nihilo, to the point that it had felt like a natural part of his experience of the world. Had any of the tattoo remained on Jackie's arm once she was buried?

"My mom's in San Fran," the woman continued. "We go out a few times a year. Do you live out there?"

"Yeah. I was in New York, visiting my sister."

"That's sweet you guys are close."

He turned to Nancy, who was asleep. They had certainly gotten closer in the last year. *New York has no associations with Jackie*, she'd said, *just come stay for a few days*. Now Cam pictured the steadier temperatures of San Francisco, how that lack of surprise could bring a stability. He thought of holding Kate somewhere along Ocean Beach. But then he thought of the water.

Cam unhooked his seat belt—he had to get up. He sat still for a moment, watching Nancy sleeping so soundly, appearing almost not to breathe. He tapped her gently on her shoulder. "Bathroom," he said. "Sorry."

She opened her eyes and stretched her neck. "Didn't you just go?"

He shrugged his shoulders.

She stared at him for a second before unclipping her seat belt.

Cam stood in line behind a stout man in a trucker hat. He didn't have to pee, but it felt good to stand, to be unbuckled. He noticed Nancy turning to check on him. He offered a limp thumbs-up and mouthed *I'm fine*.

The edge of the drink cart was visible next to the male flight attendant who'd presented the emergency instructions close to him. His blond hair was gelled and neatly parted on the side. The stack of upturned plastic cups rose like a monolith.

"Excuse me," Cam said to the man in line in front of him. He stepped up to the attendant. "Can I get a drink?"

"We're just about to bring the cart around," he said.

"Oh, OK," Cam said.

The bathroom door opened; an old woman scooched past him. The other man in line stepped inside. Cam leaned close to the attendant. "Listen," he said. "My sister is sober, and I can't let her see me drinking. All I need is one small bottle of vodka. I won't ask you for anything else."

Cam looked back at his seat; his sister was leaned over talking to the woman next to her. At first, the flight attendant didn't respond, but then he quickly reached into one of the cart's metal drawers. He handed Cam a tiny bottle.

"Thank you—seriously," Cam said. The drink's tiny size seemed to convey its inconsequence. He'd made it ten months—that counted for something. He slid it into his pocket and continued waiting for the bathroom.

He felt weightless as he walked slowly down the aisle. The plane began to shake, just, but then steadied. It took a few minutes to reach his seat, as he was trapped behind the cart.

"You sure you're OK?" Nancy asked, speaking in a whisper.

"I'm fine," Cam said. "I promise. Old age is messing with my bladder."

"I'm proud of you," she said. "I want you to know." She looked at him, with her brown, glossy eyes.

He smiled against the bleak mass of his thoughts.

"Thank you, sis," he said. "No one has come through for me like you. I know this has been hard on you too."

"You should talk about it, Cam," she said.

"What?"

"You should try opening up, unburdening yourself." She nodded next to him. "Tell her, you'll never see her again. It's practice."

He tensed. "I don't want to talk about my sobriety," he said.

"I mean Jackie."

He hated hearing her name. He knew Nancy was right. He pushed his bag further under the seat with his foot. He wanted to pull his belt out and wrap his hands in it.

He managed to doze for an hour or so. When he woke, he felt a pit in his stomach, or like he was ill.

The female flight attendant announced their initial descent. The woman next to him got Lloyd settled in her lap. "Thank you for being so sweet with him," she said. "Your son is a lucky kid."

He thanked her, nodding his head. Andrew was so far from lucky. Cam was lucky; the last year had proven this. He remembered how Jackie had loved falling asleep in the crook of Andrew's arm. For a period, she'd wanted only him to put her to bed.

Cam felt parched. He grabbed his water and took a long gulp. Once he twisted the cap closed, he spoke again. "You think you'll have another?"

The woman thought for a moment before speaking. "Maybe," she said. "He's such a handful, though."

"You should," he said. "You're already raising a great big brother."

Nancy put a hand on his forearm and left it there. Cam could feel the plane slowly change its course. He rested his head. Landing was the part he feared most. The way the sound seemed to take up physical space around him—visceral—the roar of force and speed pressing against his chest, conjuring a quick end.

In his pocket, Cam pressed the bottle between his fingers. The empty plastic made a faint cracking sound. He traced his finger around the rim.

NEW MOTION

Their room was bright when Chris woke, light filled, and the window's warmth reached him on the couch. Mitzi cradled Amos on her hospital bed. Some color had returned to her face.

"How are you feeling?" Chris squinted. Waking up again to see Amos, their son, only two days old, was miraculous.

"I feel reborn," she said. "God—I was tired." She rotated Amos to face Chris and gently held him up. "Can you believe this little creature?"

Chris rose and came over to kiss the top of Mitzi's head. A single gray strand of hair sparkled beneath his lip. Despite her having slept only a few hours, her eyes were lively. Just days before, Chris had taken a picture of Mitzi, standing at the open window of their apartment. Her belly appeared to have the power to bend whatever was around it, including the window's protective bars.

"Your dad texted," she said.

"Texted you?"

Mitzi nodded. "He was just checking in."

Mitzi had a soft spot for his dad, but Chris and Mitzi had agreed to get through the birth alone. No friends, no family. Meaning with as much ease and calm as possible. (Due to several large fibroids near her uterus, Mitzi had a cesarean, which made the process more manageable; it removed many of the unknowns and made her feel in control.) They both considered themselves mildly estranged from their immediate families, and the last time they'd seen Chris's dad, at the baby shower two months before, it had been something of a disaster. He'd had a little too much to drink, was a little too adamantly pressing to pay the remainder of the tab at the beer garden, trying to prove himself. A shouting match had ensued, and Chris's dad had stormed off. Leaving Chris mortified.

"He's here," Chris said. "I didn't tell you before. I thought I could hold him off."

"In the city?" She looked down at Amos, who burbled.

Chris nodded. Despite Chris having told his dad that they'd see him in a few days, he'd come to the city anyway. *I'm around*, he'd texted, which always gave Chris the impression that his dad was somehow everywhere, hovering.

"Maybe he should give us a ride home?"

Chris pictured himself hunched over and weeping in the empty hospital cafeteria the night before. He'd been in such a state that he'd almost called his dad.

"I know it's not what we decided," she continued, "but, Chris—I'm tired. I'd rather ride home in the car with someone we know."

Her eyes were wide, sincere. In the later months of Mitzi's pregnancy, Chris had imagined himself behind the wheel of the car en route to the hospital—maybe he'd always had this thought—but they lived in Brooklyn and had never needed a car. Chris had called the Lyft at 5:00 a.m. to leave enough time to practice installing the new car seat before they left.

"Is he really that different than a Lyft driver?" she joked.

How many times had Chris waited for his dad to pick him up over the years? At practices, from after-school care. Chris's mom, may she rest in peace, never drove. More times than he could count, a teammate's mother would take him home, or he'd wait at school with the security guard, watching the cafeteria lights turn off, which always felt somehow illicit.

Chris grabbed his phone. After several rings, his dad answered.

"Dad," Chris said.

"Chris." He cleared his throat, his voice hoarse. "How are you? How's the babe?"

"We're doing well. Last night was rough." He wondered how much he should say. "But we're doing better today." Chris switched the phone to speaker.

"Hey," Mitzi said.

"Mitz, how are you, beautiful?"

"I'm great. And Amos is great," she said.

"Wait a beat before calling me Grandpa, will you? I'm fragile."

Mitzi laughed.

Chris rolled his eyes. "We were thinking it'd be good to get home with some relative ease," he said. "Would you be able to give us a ride back to Brooklyn?"

"What happened to all the going-it-alone stuff?"

Mitzi pursed her lips.

"It's fine, never mind," Chris said. "We'll just—"

"Of course," his dad said. "I'd be happy to, just let me know what time and I'll be there."

Later that morning, as they started to pack, Chris placed Amos in the car seat for practice and fastened the belt, taking care not to snag his son in the buckle. He seesawed the seat with his toes. Amos raised an arm and curled his fingers. He was so small—five pounds, nine ounces—that the sleeves of his onesie covered his hands.

The first thing that Chris had learned about his son was that he didn't like to be still. Only movement kept him calm. Chris's hips and quads felt sore from endless bouncing.

"It would be cute if he called you Papa," Mitzi said. She wore a gray sweatshirt and flannel pajama pants. She moved tentatively. "You've been giving me *papa* vibes these last few days." She flicked her eyebrows.

Papa, he repeated in his mind several times.

"I can't wait to nest with you two," she said. "I'm so happy we're going home."

The lobby was bustling as they left. People smiled and cooed at Amos. The car seat hardly felt heavier with him in it. Mitzi walked slowly but ably, grateful to be out of their room. Outside, cabs were backed up approaching the entrance, and for a moment Chris was relieved not to be riding in one.

"Can we wait outside?" Mitzi rose up on her toes. "I'm dying for fresh air."

When they walked through the revolving door, the outside world seemed to rush at them. New York was a merciless grid. Amos rested beneath the canopy of his blanket. On the pavement,

Chris flattened the duffel bag and made a cushion for the car seat so Amos wouldn't be on the ground. Chris kneeled beside him, gazing at the street from his line of sight.

"Will you wrap the extra blanket around him?" Mitzi asked. "I can't believe he's outside, finally in the world."

Chris got Amos snug and checked his phone: 10:12. His dad was late, of course. He wondered how long a grace period he should afford him before hailing one of the many waiting cabs. Amos started to fuss; Chris rocked the seat back and forth. Mitzi stepped closer to them, and Chris carefully rubbed her back. He scanned the street.

Idling at the light was his dad's prized old Audi A4. The exhaust rose above the car's roof. He remembered when he was eleven and they'd come to Manhattan for an auto show, his dad commenting obsessively on the Audi's mileage. Chris's car sickness had built steadily. His dad told him to make like a dog and stick his head out the window to get some fresh air.

The light changed and Chris felt tense. His arms were tired from the rocking. The car's fumes were strong when his dad pulled up. Chris lifted Amos and turned him away to shield him. Chris's dad hopped out of the car in a beaten suede jacket, tortoiseshell sunglasses propped on his head. Apart from his cameo at the baby shower, it had been nine months since Chris had seen him. He and Chris didn't hug, but his dad squeezed the top of his shoulder before giving Mitzi a kiss on the cheek.

"Where's my little grandbaby-boy?" He searched Amos's face.

Chris opened the back door, and the clicking sound and the leather's roasted smell triggered more nostalgia. Weekends searching dealerships for vintage parts—radio knobs and console covers—Genesis blaring from the speakers. Chris's boredom never seemed to register. His dad still didn't get that Chris didn't give a shit about cars.

Chris realized then that someone needed to hold Amos while the seat was installed. Mitzi wasn't strong enough yet to hold him while standing.

"I've got it," his dad said.

"No, I'll do it," Chris said.

His dad peeked around the back of the car seat. "I wouldn't know where to begin with this new age gadget. Let me hold him while you do your thing, Pops."

Chris looked at Amos.

His dad noticed his hesitation and smirked. "I've done this all before, you know?" he said. "That's the only reason you're able to do it."

Chris handed Amos over, lowering him into the cradle of his father's arms. He was nervous to pull away. Chris's dad started whispering something to Amos, and Chris watched them for a minute before belting in the car seat.

By the time they reached the FDR Drive, Amos had fallen asleep. Chris and Mitzi sat together with Amos in the back. They held hands across the car seat, its sloped edges plump with foam. Mitzi's palm grew warm in Chris's as he stared from the car window at the river. He thought of the operation the day before last—when he pushed through the door to see Mitzi lying still on the table, halved by a gray curtain. Her eyes searched him as he pulled his chair in close. He told her it would all be OK, that she was doing great. The doctor came over to their side of the table with her large vintage glasses and deadpan demeanor (she was their least favorite among the trio) and asked whether or not they wanted to drop the curtain to see the operation. Mitzi had said she'd make a game-time decision, and Chris was ultimately relieved not to witness the gore. When the doctor said they were about to pull the baby free, Mitzi renewed her grip on Chris's hand; he tensed his body as if it might anchor her. He could feel the doctor pulling, and Mitzi seemed almost like an extension of him, the densest garment that had snagged on some corner and was being tugged free. Tears slid down Mitzi's cheeks. He told her she was almost there, though he didn't know if it was true until he did. Until they both did. The baby, their son, was only his screams. A wailing sound filled the room and poured deep down into their chests.

When they passed their exit on the Prospect Expressway, Chris's stomach dropped. "Dad, that was us. I told you twenty-six."

He smiled in the rearview. "I know. I'm just making a quick pit stop."

It seemed like a joke. Chris's heart beat steadily, a slow, mocking laugh. Mitzi squeezed his hand.

"You're kidding," Chris said. "We just want to get home."

"I figured I had time to sneak it in before I drop you off."

"Jesus, Dad. Make things simple for once."

"It's not far out of the way, I swear," he said. "I found this Audi parts dealer on eBay. He has the shifter knob and fog lights. Both!"

"Car parts? You're not fucking serious."

"I set this up before I knew I'd be driving you home. It will only take a sec."

Traffic began to slow. Chris watched his dad's hand resting casually on the gearshift. Trembling. Chris wanted to scream. He remembered the hot parking lot where he'd learned to drive stick shift the summer after junior year of high school. His mom had come with them, cheering from the grass as Chris, haltingly, got the hang of it. His dad had been proud of him. Chris knew his dad had been lonely—despite his dad not letting on—in the five years since his mom passed, but he'd just gotten more insufferable. He was only interested in his car, slowly rebuilding its engine after work and on the weekends and sending Chris pictures of pipes and wires he couldn't fully differentiate.

"How long before you get back in the ring?" Chris's dad asked Mitzi.

"*Ooof*," she said. "I haven't even thought about it."

Mitzi had started boxing the year before she'd gotten pregnant, working with a trainer in the park and at a boxing gym in Bay Ridge. Chris had a video of her on his phone, sparring with her eight-month-round belly, her punches still swift and sharp.

"You ever get out there and spar with her, Chris?"

"She'd whoop me," Chris said. "I'm smarter than that."

"Yeah—my money's on Mitz," his dad said.

The traffic built steadily. Despite this, Chris's dad switched lanes several times, as if he might thread his way through it. Chris rested his head against the window. He worried that Amos would start crying if they came to a stop.

A second later Chris's window began rolling down. Chris startled, jerking his head away. The air whipped in. He pressed the button, but the child lock was on. "Roll it up," he said to his father, frustrated. "The noise."

"Thought you might need some air, sheesh."

Chris's dad eyed him in the rearview.

"Mitz, you know how he gets."

Mitzi reached over to Chris and palmed his forearm. *It's OK*, she mouthed.

"Your mom used to send me out for drives to get you to sleep," he said. "You were so stubborn."

Mitzi lifted the blanket up to check on Amos, who was still asleep. The blanket's gossamer quality betrayed the heavy frustration it had already caused Chris. Failing to properly swaddle Amos had nearly broken him the first night. He'd been trying to let Mitzi sleep, but Amos kept fussing, crying. The younger nurse, with a streak of blue in her hair, had brought Chris a swaddle blanket with a Velcro strap that changed everything. Chris had looked haggard enough that she offered to take Amos to the nursery so he could sleep. He wasn't ready to go back in the room, though, so he took the elevator downstairs to the lobby, followed signs for the cafeteria. The kitchen was closed, but coffee and a few packaged snacks were available. He didn't want to face a choice then. To be so unsure of his abilities in a situation of such permanence—he wanted to be told what to do. He sat at a long empty table and pulled out his phone. Instead of dialing, he looked down at the floor, the speckled linoleum blurring and coming into focus.

Chris's dad parked outside of a small white house. He grabbed his wallet from the glove compartment.

"Hang tight," he said. "I won't be long."

When he got to the door, a man with a maroon baseball hat answered and they disappeared inside.

"I'm sorry I suggested this," Mitzi said.

"It's not your fault—he's completely oblivious. He couldn't have done this later?"

"I know," she said. "It's crazy."

"He's so fucking selfish—this is exactly why I didn't want him involved." Chris was almost yelling, and Amos started to cry. Chris peeled back the blanket, feeling foolish for allowing himself to get worked up, for letting it affect Amos. He tried to rock the seat, to get Amos back to sleep, but there wasn't much give with the seat belt. He grabbed the edge and violently shook the car seat.

"Stop, Chris," Mitzi said.

He didn't listen.

"Please, just calm down."

He couldn't take the sound of saliva quivering in Amos's throat, the rattle. He undid the buckle and scooped Amos out. Mitzi looked away, out the window toward the house, as he opened the door and got out. Chris cradled Amos's head on his shoulder, the timbre of the little cries tickling the wax in Chris's ears. He wrapped his son in the blanket and tucked the long stray corner into the front, only to see it come undone as he lifted Amos. The blanket fell to the sidewalk. Amos cried louder. Chris bounced, bounced more deeply still, and dipped to snatch the blanket from the ground with the tips of his fingers. He squeezed Amos hard against his body in frustration. He realized suddenly the danger of what he'd just done. They'd been warned repeatedly in class about curtailing these spontaneous bursts of aggression. His heart pounded and his eyes watered. Amos cried anew, the reverberations from his cries like different sorts of cries that might amount to an infinite sound.

Chris walked further up the block. Sweat pricked the crown of his head. His calves strained. The wind blew across them. Above him, a cloud quickly made way for the sun. He started to sway. Amos was calming, he could feel it. He'd be OK once they were back on the road. Chris continued up the sidewalk, away from the car, his dad. The sun's warmth soothed his neck and shoulders. He turned away to shield his son from it. Once they reached the corner, Chris closed his eyes to try to settle his heart rate. For a moment all was calm.

After several minutes, he took a deep breath and walked back to the car. His dad was leaving the house. He was carrying a white plastic bag and sporting a grin.

"I got something for you," he said.

"Oh?" Chris said wryly.

Mitzi got out of the car and took Amos.

"For you three, actually." His dad held up a single key hanging from a leather key chain. It twisted slowly in the air.

Chris and Mitzi looked at each other, bewildered.

"She's right over here." He walked several cars away to a small white Audi that Chris knew was an A2. "Not quite vintage yet, but there's only fifty thousand miles on it. I hope you'll add some coming to visit me."

Chris was stunned. He'd never expected to own a car in New York—never expected to own a car at all. The parking was brutal near their building. It didn't feel like a gift. "Dad—you didn't have to do this."

Mitzi walked over and hugged Chris's dad. "I can't believe it." She spoke softly to Amos then. "What do you think, bud? Our family car."

Chris rubbed his face, shocked that he'd be driving a car home. As his dad popped the trunk, Amos turned and stared at Chris. His tiny eyes looked shifty. Chris felt like he saw a flash of personality, of attitude, and almost laughed. He stepped in close, looking at the deep, unspeakable blue of Amos's pupils. The dark eddies of his hair and the creases in his delicate little face as if all freshly scored. Chris's son. Many years later, Amos would sit in the passenger seat, his hair mussed by the highway wind.

STERLING

Most mornings, I woke up beside a beheaded *Paw Patrol* toy. It was Chase, Sterling always reminded me, the police officer dog. I'd tried to fix it about a month before, with the wrong kind of glue, but then I got used to it there on the nightstand. In pieces.

Sterling used to ask about it every morning, but even he, at six years old, had given up. A true stepfather should be able to fix it, if that's what I ever hoped to be.

I'd been spending more nights with Leslie, my girlfriend, though I still felt tentative about it, like I was a roommate. Their house was huge—a prewar D.C. townhome with three stories. Leslie worked as a cardiologist at Children's National Hospital. We'd met online; she'd warned me, beyond her limited schedule, that she and Sterling were a package deal. I'd never considered being a father figure so young, or living with a kindergartener, though I worked part-time at a tutoring center with kids of all ages. My income was modest, if stable. I said I was open to it if she was, and our relationship had since grown more serious. The second time I came to the house, I'd met Sterling, hiding behind his mother's leg—gap-toothed with a broccoli top. He'd asked his mom, failing to whisper, "Who is this man?" At twenty-eight, I still didn't consider myself one.

"Duuuuude," a voice called out. It grew louder as it ascended the steps.

"Stir-crazy," I replied.

"I told you: don't call me that."

"I'm sorry—*Sterling*."

Recently, Sterling's curiosity had given way to full-blown entitlement. He didn't even crack the bedroom door and ask if he could come in first. I wasn't about to have a conversation about boundaries with a six-year-old.

"What should we do?" he asked.

There was so much I should be doing: The director at the tutoring center had asked me to fill in for a board member on parental leave. Taking meeting notes, sending follow-ups and summaries—more practice for the real thing, she said. A position among the professional managerial class felt like a death knell.

Sterling rolled his eyes when I didn't respond with actionable ideas. He hung from the loose doorknob, which had long since become redundant, and called me boring. He looked around the room. "Bro," he said. "You're messy."

A moment later Leslie came upstairs. She stood in the doorway in plum-colored scrubs, which grabbed along her thighs. "Fifteen minutes, Sterling. No more." She glared at her son and then at me with her hazel eyes.

I'd started to watch Sterling when Leslie was on call. This typically meant the afternoons and early evenings, which didn't conflict with my work schedule. In truth, I enjoyed it more than I'd expected to.

Sterling mentioned his dad infrequently, but after he met my own dad (in passing and in an unavoidable fashion), he'd brought him up several times. I stopped myself from saying that dads were typically dubious men—that mine, despite the quick charm he displayed in dodging his hand slaps out on the front steps, was no different.

Leslie had detailed her ex's failings; he'd cheated shortly after Sterling was born and now lived in Wisconsin, where he'd already fathered another child. Sterling had been so young he didn't have someone to miss, she said. Leslie was grateful they hadn't been married, though she struggled to receive adequate child support from him. She didn't know that my dad still paid me a monthly stipend, even though he hadn't been required to by law for over ten years. My mom said I should continue accepting the money as long as I could, that this was an extension of her own restitution. She'd moved to Sarasota when I'd gone to college, claiming that my dad was so embedded in D.C. it was impossible to remain in the city without constant reminders of his arrogance and philandering. Just look at the branded scaffolding at any newly erected property. I sometimes told people he was a slumlord when they asked, just for the fuck of it. He'd been a developer for almost forty years.

Late the next night, Leslie sat curled on the living room couch. Her whole body seemed twisted carefully to support the glass of Pinot in her hand. This was a me'vening, as she called them—important affairs for a single mother. I almost hadn't noticed her on my way out.

"What's nightlife like, again?" Her hair was postshower neat, hanging.

"That's one way to describe it." I didn't drink, and tonight I was heading out to see my friend George as he set up a DIY art space for a gallery show. This meant helping him avoid calamity as he drank whiskey while operating power tools.

"Stop trying to act like you're so much older than me. Seven years isn't much." I sat down. "How was work?"

She closed her eyes, opened them again slowly. A shadow lay across her freckled clavicle. "Had a tracheal rupture come in this afternoon," she said. "The girl almost died."

Small talk with her was impossible. The patient had been just a year older than Sterling. "Almost is a win," I said.

Leslie took a sip and undid her legs. "I want you to know how much Sterling enjoys you. I see him opening up."

Sterling had been closed off at first, clinging to his mom whenever the three of us were together. I'd resorted to pratfalls and potty humor to soften him.

"We were eating breakfast the other day and he started telling me about socialism."

When I grinned, she rolled her eyes.

"I balked, but then hearing him talk it through so innocently made me emotional. It's an uncanny thing to see another person living in your child's voice, their spirit."

Whenever Leslie reported back the things Sterling had said, telling me how he'd relayed some bit of trivial information or a fleeting opinion I'd expressed, I felt I offered some genuine value. Like my thoughts and beliefs would live on in him.

Before I left, I looked back at the house from the sidewalk. One of the first times I'd babysat Sterling, we'd read Dr. Seuss's *Ten Apples Up on Top!* together, and he'd fallen asleep before the cart exploded and everyone got an even share of the fruit. I'd wanted to tell him what it meant, what it all meant. As he was closing his eyes, he'd traced his small finger in circles around the lower joint of my thumb, almost without knowing it. Now, he was wading through whatever thoughts a six-year-old had before falling asleep. When I was a kid, I used to have a glass of seltzer beside my bed even though I rarely drank from it. My dad was typically gone at night, though I could hear his voice muffled through the door sometimes. I vowed to fix Sterling's toy the next day.

The space was littered with shipping pallets and other industrial scraps when I arrived. George sat amid a wreckage of wood. I lifted a medium-size canvas off the ground; it depicted a large oval just barely touching a smaller one. Curiously accomplished.

He moved his glasses up his nose with a finger. "That's mine." His blond-dyed hair was growing out, dark at the roots. He was an incredible painter, deeply conflicted about what success in art meant (one of the many reasons I respected him). "It's OK to pad out the show with your work," I said.

"The other stuff is good—please!"

I tilted the canvas back against the wall. "I'm sorry your talent is a burden. At least it's yours to bear." On the floor stood a not-quite-empty Jameson bottle. "Let's cheers to it."

He loved a ceremony, so I grabbed two plastic cups from the back and filled mine with water. We tapped rims and swigged.

"You ever think we'd be pushing thirty and slumming it in a DIY space?" He squeezed his eyes closed and held them, as if to evoke pain.

"I can't take you wavering right now—not here," I comically pleaded. "Not like this."

We'd been friends since high school and had found ourselves in similar places of late-twenties aimlessness.

"Your dad sent me an email," he said. "I'll never stop thanking you for this."

My dad had brokered a deal with the owners of the building; they'd offered a lease to George's organization at a discounted rate (the space had sat vacant for nearly a year). The man was only one degree removed from everyone who owned anything in the city. Everything he did was a ploy. All I'd done was call him.

"Have you seen him lately?"

I hadn't, though he was overdue for a dinner.

"How's the pseudo-family?" he asked.

George knew these types of comments got to me. He was fond of Sterling too, but less convinced of my relationship with Leslie. To him I was a glorified babysitter.

"You have to bring Sterling to the opening," he said. "He'll love it."

George had given Sterling paint-by-numbers sheets of famous works. He was convinced of Sterling's nascent genius, which made me excited to imagine. The opening would be good for Sterling, envisioning his work up on some future wall. Leslie often worried when we ventured too far from home, but there were exceptions.

As we walked home from school, Sterling told me about a kid in his class who'd left the school to go to a corner store for snacks. The boy's dad had been called in. He'd been upset.

"Aren't there vending machines in school?" I asked.

"Yeah, but they don't have Little Debbie." Bright green paint had stained Sterling's pinkie and palm.

"You better not pull some shit like that."

He grimaced and said *aw*.

"Sorry—*stuff*."

He was hungry. Constantly. But I wanted to show him something first. He gently resisted before agreeing to walk down Fourteenth Street with me. We passed the dive that made the Tater Tots Sterling loved, and on the next block was a new mural by one of the artists in George's show. It lined a high school soccer field on a low wall of vibrant color; simple geometric shapes zigzagged the length, some of them looking like tiny figures. When we arrived, Sterling ran his pointer finger across as if testing the dryness of the paint. His eyes widened and he said the mural looked like Keith. I almost said "Keith who?" before I realized he meant Keith Haring. Sterling's mind was stunning sometimes.

"Do you even like color?" he asked. "You only wear black."

"I can appreciate it, but that doesn't mean I want to dress like a Jolly Rancher."

He tried not to smile. When we reached Twelfth Street, I turned down the hill toward Florida Ave. He pulled at my hand and claimed starvation.

"Be patient," I said. "I'll buy you anything you want."

"A vape?" he said.

"What's wrong with you?"

"Don't say *anything* then. You're not the boss of me."

"Anything edible—that's not destructive to your health."

Florida Ave was scattered with pedestrians. Sterling was excited to point out another small mural, attached to a moderate condo of modern complexion. One of my dad's properties. Duke Ellington sat at a billowing ribbon of piano keys, and I tried to explain the difference between public and private art: which was for us and which was for profit. He wanted snacks, not food for thought. A cookie in particular.

"Can we go to District Grind?" he asked.

Another new eyesore.

"Please? Their salted oatmeal cookies are the best."

I didn't have the fight—he was six.

"I'll give you money," I said, "but I'm not going inside."

"What's wrong with *you*?" he asked.

"A ton." I handed him five dollars.

I was hoping dinner would be at a restaurant, but last minute my dad asked me to come by his place. (This, at the very least, precluded waitresses.) He lived in a penthouse in a tall building overlooking U Street that he'd renovated years before. His kitchen was huge, immaculate thanks to its infrequency of use. Copper countertops spread in all directions and opened onto a large living room. He'd ordered from a new Indonesian place nearby and arranged our shallow bowls on the island. He wore a white Henley with the buttons undone; it hugged tight to his bulging midsection. His hair was longer now, light gray and wavy.

"I was thinking of stopping by the opening." He sucked a finger clean before rinsing it in the sink.

His attendance was an empty gesture he felt held the weight of currency. It wasn't inconceivable that he'd show up, blending in with whatever low-budget version of New York's art elite D.C.'s pretended to be.

"George is impressive for all he's managed to do," he said. "You were in college together?"

"High school," I said.

We chewed in silence for a bit.

"How's work?" he asked. "How does it feel to be in on the board meetings?"

"I'm only responsible for a few more months. Looking forward to it being over, to be honest."

"Executive directors at nonprofits make decent money. It might be a good idea to take this a bit more seriously."

I'd heard this before, naturally. And not only from him; from Leslie too. "I like interacting with the kids. I don't want to get alienated from the part I enjoy."

"What about your life?"

"What about it?" I asked.

He took a slow sip of his wine. "How much longer are you going to play dad?"

"I thought we agreed not to talk about this?"

"I'm worried," he said. "I don't like the idea of you raising another man's son."

"Why? I enjoy it."

"You're sacrificing a potential career. How long am I supposed to subsidize your ennui?" The tiny edge of his collar shook as his knee bounced against his stool. "You're almost thirty. That may seem an arbitrary number to you but it's not."

I began to feel the typical pinch across my chest. I was determined to stay calm. On a nearby shelf, I saw the picture of my dad and me from my eighteenth birthday, courtside at a Wizards game. I hated sports, but he'd been so excited to be so close to the action there.

"I wish you'd give some thought to the Res Dev stuff," he said. His voice had slowed down, and he spoke quietly, which was rare. His company's Responsible Development initiative partnered with community organizations to *offset* the cost of gentrification.

"I wouldn't be any good at it," I said.

"Don't be ridiculous, you'd be excellent. I honestly think you could run it on your own."

I thought about it for the briefest of moments, as I did whenever he mentioned it. I saw myself seated behind a comically large desk.

"You could work with people, with kids. The point is: you could do whatever you want. And you'd start at six figures."

"I can't do a job I don't believe in. What use would that be to anyone?"

"Who says you're supposed to enjoy what you do? Who says that's something you're entitled to? Your generation is something else."

I remained silent.

"Whether you like it or not, I'm paying part of your way still, so even if you're morally or ideologically opposed to the work, you're benefiting from it. This little kid is benefiting, shit." He got up suddenly and poured himself more wine. "I'm cutting you off at thirty. It's embarrassing. Ultimately I'm enabling you."

"Fine." I gripped the edge of my stool.

He tilted back the last sip of his wine. A tiny scarlet droplet fell to his shirt, seeping and pink. I could tell he was already becoming drunk.

"We'll see how long you manage to live out this fantasy."

I tried to do a quick tally in my mind, imagining how much pressure I could bear once he withdrew the monthly financial commitment. I could still pay my rent for a bit; I'd be fine. I'd pitch in more with Sterling.

"You don't have to decide this minute," he said, as if realizing the futility. "I get worked up because I care, you know."

"Your view of success is narrow." As I spoke, I wasn't sure if I was tempting a retort out of him or whether I just wanted to get a final word in.

"At least I have a view."

Leslie stood in the kitchen, tipping powder into a stout pot of mac and cheese. This was Sterling's main source of protein. He was upstairs playing Roblox on his iPad.

She read the surprise on my face to see her makeup. "Don't make me self-conscious."

"You look beautiful," I said.

She turned around to grab the pot with her gloved grip, and I watched her shoulder blades through her large T-shirt.

"I don't feel like being *on* tonight," she said.

She was going to a hospital fundraiser. Donors, drinks, and drudgery, she'd said. "Try and enjoy yourself. This counts as a nightlife."

"How was your dad?"

I grasped for words. "Good, fine." *Fine and good*, I thought.

She covered the bowl with tinfoil. "Well, I appreciate you," she said. "Even if his dumb ass struggles to."

I stepped close to her and gave her a hug.

"I have to get dressed. Make sure Sterling's in bed no later than nine. I doubt I'll be too late."

When she was out of sight, I snuck a bite of the still-warm noodles.

I went up to Sterling's room to check on him. He was on his back, the screen pressed to his nose.

"You're gonna go blind," I said.

He didn't respond.

I stepped over and grabbed the device. He writhed like I'd snatched a vital organ.

"We're doing something different tonight," I said.

"What?" He dropped his brow.

"We're gonna go to the gallery."

"I want to stay hoooooome."

"We'll just go for a bit." I rushed to pack. Leslie wouldn't be back before ten.

Sterling sighed.

"Please, just trust me."

He looked at me with a tinge of fear. I kneeled in front of him.

"Fine," he said. "But I'm bringing Chase."

"He's still broken," I said.

"I know— I'll put him in my backpack."

We waited for the bus on a low wall of unsteady bricks. An old woman ambled past in a bucket hat, and when she smiled at us I nodded, accepting her kindest assumption. Sterling knocked his heels against the wall, impatient. I'd never taken the bus as a kid. But I'd always imagined how it would feel not being driven around all the time. Almost like equals with my parents. Two years ago I'd taken the preliminary courses and written exam to become a city bus driver. My dad thought I was joking when I'd mentioned it (the potential six-figure salary hadn't been convincing enough). His skepticism functioned as temporary motivation; I'd bailed before the first driving test.

When the bus pulled up, Sterling jumped out of its way theatrically and then hopped up on one foot when the doors sighed open. He was livelier now. The two back corner seats were ours, a glossy Lego blue. His feet dangled; he was wearing those yellow perforated sneakers he loved. The ride would be less than ten minutes, but he asked immediately for my phone. I said *absolutely*. And then *not*. He frowned and looked out the window.

A crowd had gathered outside the show, composed mostly of teenagers. Dyed hair and dark clothes. Safety pins. This was one of few occasions when I thought it appropriate to ditch my black T-shirt for a black button-up. Sterling grabbed my hand as we approached.

Inside, the space was better lit than I'd ever seen it, the floors sprawling and clean. Precisely placed paintings activated the room with color. Everyone had a clear cup in their hand, and suddenly Sterling was thirsty. He stayed close to my side. We walked to a cloth-covered table tended by a teenager in a T-shirt and sheer vest. Then Sterling decided he was hungry too. I'd left the zippered pouch of snacks on the kitchen counter.

We ordered seltzer waters, and George found us soon.

"Sterling!" he said. "You made it."

I held Sterling's cup as they bumped fists.

"Come," George said. "I've got so much to show you."

Sterling followed him tentatively. I needed a place to set down the bag, so I went back to George's makeshift office and slid it under his desk. I noticed my dad's business card resting exactly at the midpoint in front of his computer monitor. The same rounded edges and bright white card stock from when I was a kid. I set my cup of seltzer under the desk lamp. The water popped and fizzed, the tiny bubbles exploding. I closed my eyes and could almost hear it. My mom had tried to stop him, but he'd stumbled through the door, bringing the hallway's brightness with him. I'd been pretending to sleep when he sat clumsily beside me. His weight sloped me toward him. He smelled bitter, smoky. I'm not sure if he even noticed the water already on my bedside table, but he placed the second glass down beside it. A small spill collected at the base. He grabbed me and hugged me, laughing under his breath. When I tried to get free, he grabbed me tighter. I had trouble breathing, but he seemed to think it was a game. My mom was in the doorway, telling him to stop. I panicked, which finally caused me to go slack. He let me go and raked his thick fingers through my hair. After he left, a chill spread across my body. It took some time for my heart to settle down. I watched the spilled water slowly set in and stain the dark wood before falling asleep.

The gallery was packed when I came back out of the office. The crowd was a mix of drab jumpsuits and Brooks Brothers, Doc Martens and heels. I slid flat ice chips from my cup into my mouth and chewed as I pretended to scrutinize the art.

When I checked my phone, I saw that Leslie had texted several times. She'd decided to leave the fundraiser early and wondered if we were at the park. I typed back that we'd stopped by George's show. A moment later my phone rang.

"Why didn't you tell me you were going?"

"We're coming back soon, just stopping by." I ducked into a corner of the room, nodding at a woman I recognized from a local arts foundation.

"I didn't ask that. You can't just take my son off somewhere without letting me know."

"I'm sorry."

"What were you thinking?"

"Leslie, we're coming back."

She breathed heavily into the phone.

"I thought he'd be inspired," I said.

"He's six!" she said.

"I know."

"Just please get him home, OK?"

"OK."

I sped through the space. My heart rate rose when I couldn't find him. I did two loops before finally spotting George.

"Where's Sterling?"

"He went with your dad."

I stared at him. "What?"

"He kept saying he was hungry, and your dad had come over to say hey. He offered to take him," he said. "I didn't know what to do. I figured you knew."

My mind spun out.

"He's bringing him right back," George said. "They went to District Grind, I think."

I tossed my cup at a trash can, and it missed, popping on the concrete floor. Outside it was starting to get dark. A breeze blew my dress shirt against my body; it suddenly felt as big as a bedsheet. In front of the coffee shop, a short man in an apron folded down the blackboard sign. They were closing soon.

I saw Sterling and my dad through the window. Black turtleneck and blazer. When he noticed me, my dad looked as if he'd been expecting this.

"What are you doing?" I asked.

Sterling ate a salted oatmeal cookie with a crumb-laden lip.

"Kiddo said he was hungry."

His bloodshot eyes looked poisonous.

"He's got good taste."

My dad palmed Sterling's small, curly head. I eyed his large fingers and couldn't bring myself to sit down.

"You forgot my snacks," Sterling said, refusing to look at me. Leslie would see the snack bag on the kitchen counter.

My dad eyed me and then the table. His fist rested beside a tiny ringed glass of white wine.

"Sterling, let's go," I said. "Time to head home."

"I'm not done." He seemed defiant. I wondered what my dad had said to him.

"Now," I said.

"Hey. *Hey*." My dad's voice bore a hint of comedy. "Let him finish. He's starving."

"So a cookie was a good idea?"

My dad guffawed, hanging his head. “I’m not sure any of this was a good idea.” He sat for a minute without speaking. Sterling’s heel clunked against the leg of his chair. “We’ve been here for all of ten minutes,” he said. “I was looking for you, but I happened to run into him first. I figured he’d eventually lead me back to you.”

“You’re both wearing black,” Sterling said, unbidden.

My dad looked at my untucked shirt. I reached for Sterling’s shoulder and tried to guide him off the chair, but my dad held him back.

“He’s nearly done,” he said.

The tart perfume of his breath. “I have another event on the waterfront. I’m heading across town anyway, don’t worry.”

When Sterling crumpled the cookie’s wax bag, I grabbed it and threw it out. I took his hand as he slid off his chair.

On the sidewalk, my dad pulled out his keys and aimed them across the street. Yellow lights flashed in an illegal spot.

“I’ll give you two a ride,” he said. “Hop in.”

“We’re taking the bus,” I said.

“*Come* on,” he said. “It’s ten minutes.”

Sterling looked up at me. I didn’t move.

I stared in the direction of the bus stop and worried how long the bus would take. Sterling tried to loosen my grip on his hand.

My dad kneeled in front of him. "Thanks for keeping me company, kid," he said. He held his broad palm out, and Sterling slapped it. A small bit of cookie was still wedged in Sterling's teeth as he smiled.

Before the bus arrived, I realized that I'd forgotten the bag in George's office, realized it was too late to go back (Sterling would ask for his toy). Leslie texted asking for an ETA, which I optimistically put at fifteen minutes. After another ten, the bus pulled up. This time, as we got on, Sterling sat alone in a row of two seats. He leaned his forehead against the window. I reached across the aisle and failed to tempt him with my phone.

The bus inched toward Fourteenth Street. I checked my phone again. Traffic had slowed suddenly. For a moment I regretted declining my dad's offer for a ride.

When the bus moved, it did so only to make way. We sat in place for several minutes as the sound of a police car whooped behind us. And then another. Sterling plugged his ears dramatically, and I watched the lights continue past. I pulled out my phone and called Leslie.

"We're on the bus, but there's traffic. We're just sitting."

She sighed. "Let me speak to Sterling."

I handed over the phone. Sterling replied with single words. I watched him nod as he spoke a *yes*.

He handed me back the phone, but Leslie had hung up. I looked out of the window again. My shoulders ached. The traffic around us had come to a standstill. The sound of sirens was faint, but the color of their lights flashed in the distance. After another five minutes or so the bus resumed its route, merging slowly into traffic. An old man beside the driver sucked his teeth and threw his hands up. As we made our way down the street, through the bus's front window I saw that the lights were issuing from the median before the turn onto U Street.

I walked to the front of the bus to get a better look. Two cars were wedged together, blocking most of the eastbound traffic. An ambulance was there, its rear doors open; it must have come from the opposite direction. The red car's airbags had released, and there was a spill of glass on the ground. The other car was the same Lexus my dad had, but I couldn't see anyone in it. My heart raced, and I searched for him, worried that he was inside the ambulance. A second later I saw the gurney pop up, and a young woman's profile. Along the curb, a police car was parked, an officer pacing beside it. I noticed the man then, much younger than my dad, seated and cuffed near the cop's feet. He was trying to talk to the officer—pink blue, pink blue stuttering on his cheek. His face made a desperate performance under the lights.

When the bus lurched forward, I nearly lost my balance. I grabbed the cold metal pole and turned to see Sterling in his seat. He was still looking out of his window in the back, his tiny eyelids blinking. We were about to pass the scene on his side, seconds from a clear view. The bus picked up speed. I froze momentarily. "Sterling!" I yelled.

He turned to me with the rest of the bus, even the driver, all staring in surprise. I felt stuck. "I just remembered." I steadied myself on an empty seat back before walking toward him.

The fractured light from the cop car filled the bus. "I forgot the backpack."

He looked confused, then unconcerned. The lights glowed against his hair. "Chase is broken anyway."

I sat down in the vacant seat next to him. "I'll get the bag and fix him tomorrow, I swear." Through the window, I saw the man again, sunken on the curb.

FEEDERS

The night before we met with Babette, Sarah and I had almost canceled the interview due to stress. At the time, our daughter, Sophie, was just three months old and refused to take the bottle. Sarah had had no trouble breastfeeding her, but Sophie rebuffed the synthetic nipples, despite the many sizes and flows we'd ordered. Our night nurse had been no help, and Babette sensed our distress. When we told her about the cause, she responded, very plainly, that it was a phase that would soon pass; she asked us if she could give it a try (she was older than every other nanny we'd interviewed and seemed wise for it). Sarah handed Sophie over to Babette, and she cradled Sophie in her lap. She dragged the bottle's nipple across Sophie's lip and lifted it away, almost teasingly. After about thirty seconds Sophie latched. Sarah and I sat in the chairs opposite our baby in disbelief. Babette left and we offered her the job the next day.

It took Babette time to get used to the sprawl of our Tribeca loft. I'd also been surprised by the space when I moved in (Sarah owned it). The high ceilings, the industrial-grade kitchen, and the twice-a-week cleaner. Sarah was adopted—one of six siblings—

and her family money was old, from cardboard manufacturing. She'd been the only child to be involved with the business, pioneering a sustainability packaging program and founding the family's philanthropic organization, where I worked as communications director. I'd never dated someone so wealthy before, and I often resented how unconcerned she was with the finances. I'd grown up solidly middle-class in Baltimore—my dad waited tables at a high-end steak house, and my mom worked as a public school administrator. Even then, I'd been considered wealthy by some.

There came a point in my relationship with Sarah when I had to accept that I too was rich. After all, the money might become mine at some point, albeit partially. I'd felt like a fraud proposing to her, and then signing the prenup. The pageantry of my kneeling before her family's standing. Accepting that this rarefied life was mine, and that, really, I didn't have to work for anyone else ever again, was unsettling at first. I felt an acute guilt bearing my mom's passive-aggressive comments. And oddly, this was the moment when Moses, Sarah's gray tabby cat (to whom I was deeply allergic yet had built a painstaking immunity over the course of a year) attacked my feet. Whenever I left the bathroom after a shower, he'd hiss and pounce on my bare toes. As if he'd sniffed out an old fear of mine. As a kid, I'd had dreams about small creatures—opossums, squirrels, and beavers—assailing my toes. I was convinced Moses had penetrated my psychology, pegged me as an intruder. This was a lifestyle he too enjoyed, and he was protecting it. He ate from an automatic feeder that was double the price of my espresso machine.

When Moses took immediately to Babette, it felt like a betrayal in both directions. Since I'm also employed by Sarah's family, Babette and I shared a strange kind of kinship. Both on the payroll. Both enjoyed benefits. Both had to be wary of occasional reprimand. Babette also had a cousin in Baltimore, so she knew where I was from. And she'd been surprised that I knew anything about where she was from—Guyana—and that I loved West Indian food. It wasn't long before she insisted on teaching me how to make roti. Sometimes she stayed late and we cooked together. Roti had become a staple of our kitchen and Sophie's favorite food.

The best part of my day was Sophie running to the door when I came home from work. "Daddyyyyyyyyyyyyy," she said, clobbering my knees. Babette had put Sophie's golden hair up in two violet butterfly clips. She looked older.

Babette came over with a small snack bowl in hand; she'd been slow to rise from the couch. She wore an Atlantic City T-shirt. "This girl is getting so smart, I tell you."

As I hoisted Sophie up, she promptly squeezed my nose.

"How was your day, Jordan?" Babette asked.

Jordan isn't my name. I stood bouncing Sophie for a moment and looked at Babette, waiting for her to realize. I thought maybe even Sophie would. "Good," I said. "I was eager to get home to this little *stinker*."

The moment to correct her about my name quickly passed.

"You need a ride tonight?" Babette asked.

On Tuesday nights, I played in a pickup basketball game with friends at a high school in Sunnyside, Queens, where I used to live. She lived close to the neighborhood.

A moment later, the front door opened. Sarah came in from work. She moved cautiously, and I wondered if this was because we'd just found out she was pregnant again. (We hadn't told anyone.)

"Mommmmmy." Sophie shimmied down and ran to the door.

"Hi, Sarah," Babette said, yawning.

"Hello, everyone," Sarah said. She slipped off her shoes and took Sophie into her arms. She leaned over, and I kissed her cheek, tasting the sweat from her Orangetheory class.

I watched Babette again to see if she might realize, having now said Sarah's name, that she'd mistaken mine. But she walked into the living room to pick up stray toys from the floor. She tossed Sophie's alligator into the large patterned basket in a tall arc.

"Maybe you should let me in your basketball game," she said to me.

Her own laughter had a way of crowding out mine, especially in response to her own jokes. It was a laughter that seemed too harsh for her. I remembered basketball practices when I'd have to switch to guard taller players in the post, hearing them yell to the gym, *I've got a mouse in the house*.

"My mom used to come and watch me play," I said. "I could use a fan in the stands."

I went to the bedroom to grab my gym bag. Before we left the apartment, Babette reached down to line Sarah's shoes up with the rest of her heels by the door. Moses walked over and brushed his body against Babette's arm as she did.

In her car, an air freshener dangled from the rearview next to some Diwali beads.

"How's the family?" I asked.

Babette bumped the steering wheel with the butt of her hand. "My granddaughter got another ticket. And she didn't show up to the hearing last time. Now I have to take her in. A pain, I tell you."

She had two teenage granddaughters, one about to graduate high school.

"Girls are sweet when they're young," she continued. "Then they grow up and you wish you had boys. But then you remember that boys become men and you're glad again that you had girls." She laughed to herself. She wore her glasses when she drove and sat up close to the wheel.

"You never wanted a son?" I asked.

"My daughter was plenty for me." She smiled to herself. "I know Sarah is pregnant."

I turned and eyed her. "How?"

"A mother just knows," she said. "You want a boy? Momma's gonna need an heir." She cackled.

We crossed the Fifty-Ninth Street Bridge, which was lovely in the evening, offering a dusk-gilded view of the city. As we got deeper into the backstreets of Queens, a calm came over me, the residential blocks reminding me of neighborhoods in Baltimore—Pigtown and Butchers Hill—the Formstone fronts and the large swaths of sky rising above the roofs. It was like being dropped off for practice again.

Babette sighed before speaking. "My husband had his hours cut at work. I'm so grateful I have you all. He is too. I don't think I tell you enough."

Her husband worked as a janitor at a yeshiva in Queens. Babette had said that the Jews paid him well.

"I'm so sorry, Babette," I said. "I remember how hard it was on my mom when my dad had his hours cut when I was in high school. Will your husband look for another job? Or part-time work?"

"He's hoping it's just temporary, a few weeks. But he's definitely open to other things."

I told her I would ask around in the meantime. Before I got out of the car, she patted me twice on the forearm. "Good luck on the court!"

Later in the week, we assembled Sophie's dinner as a family. Sophie sat on the lip of the counter, scooching her butt on the marble.

"Iwanroti," she said.

"We can't eat roti every day, sweetie," Sarah said.

"Why?" Sophie frowned.

"Because we need variety in our diets." Sarah chopped broccoli florets with a large knife. Her blond hair draped her face just below her chin. She looked beautiful, if a little severe, after a long day. "It's more of a snack, not real food."

"It's real food, sweetie." I pinched Sophie's knee. I could feel Sarah's blue eyes resting on me. "It's just the more you eat something, the more likely it is that you'll turn into it!" I pinched harder, and she leaned over giggling.

As Sophie sat with her dinner, Sarah and I drank Malbec on the couch, her glass filled with a demure new pregnancy splash. Before long, Sophie grew restless again. We told her to sit in her tiny chair until she was done, which she rarely did, even with *Cocomelon* on the TV. Instead, she spread out on the couch behind the table. With her butt angled high in the air, she planted her cheek on the cushion and watched.

"It's almost bath time, stinky butt," I said.

When she didn't respond I crept over to her and stared at eye level. "What are you doing lying down like this?"

"Resting my ear," she said. "Like Babette."

Sarah set her glass down; we stared at each other for a moment.

"What, honey?" Sarah asked.

I tilted my head at her. "What do you mean?"

"Resting my ear like Babette does," she repeated. After a minute, she grew bored by our questions and flipped over onto her back. I nuzzled my head into her stomach, and she laughed uncontrollably. We continued playing as Sarah cleared Sophie's plate and went to start the bath.

When Sophie was down for bed, Sarah and I spoke quietly in the kitchen.

"What do you think Sophie meant earlier?" Sarah asked.

I lacked a sound explanation. But then I remembered. "Babette called me Jordan the other day."

She looked confused. "What do you mean?"

"Like it was my name. I thought she was making a basketball joke since it was Tuesday, but I think she just forgot."

"Stockton I can see, but Jordan, babe?" She grinned. "Did you say something?"

I shook my head. Moses sat upright in the corner and stared, which he did constantly, to unnerving effect. "I waited too long and then it felt awkward."

"And how does it feel now?"

Sarah was quick, and her playful rebukes always made me laugh. She poured me more wine.

"I bet it was the name of the guy she used to work for," I said. "She's old. She's bound to slip up."

"Resting her ear," Sarah spoke to herself. "It must be something Babette said. Bizarre."

At work several days later, I received a video clip from Sarah out of the blue. I assumed, at first, that it was her trying to be sexy in the way she'd started lately; a brief striptease or view of her bare thighs below the table. Her confidence was intoxicating. These clips had a way of landing at the most inopportune times of the day, which only added to their power. But this one wasn't sexual. Only when I started playing it did I see Moses in the frame. His triad nose darted at the camera, and I realized it was the view from his feeder. It had a camera and came with an app, too, but we'd never reviewed any footage or cued up the live feed; I'd forgotten about the capability. Then I saw Babette and Sophie in the background. Babette was seated on the couch, and Sophie was on the floor playing with her stuffed alligator. The view was partially grainy, and it glitched every few seconds. I felt like a depraved voyeur as I watched, yet I couldn't stop. Gradually, Babette began to lean. She caught herself once and sat upright before slouching over again. My heart sank to watch Sophie on the floor, playing alone. Soon enough, behind her, Babette was completely horizontal. I rewound and watched it again. I realized then that the clip's sound was off, but I couldn't bear to add any more information to what I saw. Sophie dropped her alligator and rose from the floor. When she leaned over the couch, Babette startled and sat up. They appeared to talk for a minute, and then Babette hugged Sophie. And then it was done.

That night, Sarah and I divided the evening routine. I read Sophie her favorite book about a penguin's first day of school, imagining what it would be like once Sophie started preschool next year, when Babette would have to watch two kids.

When I came out, Sarah nodded at me, holding up a bottle of white. Her face shone with snail mucin.

I nodded, and she came over to join me on the couch. "I'm shocked," she said.

"I can tell."

"You're not?"

"I am."

"Well your energy is off," she said.

"It's just that . . . I felt uncomfortable watching the video."

"No shit— We agree on that."

I pressed my lips against the glass. "Isn't it illegal to spy on someone?"

"Please. We're all spied on, all the time. It's practically nationally sanctioned," she said. "You do understand what it is you saw? Sophie was playing alone while Babette was passed out beside her."

"I know."

"I thought you'd be a tad more worried by it. There's no way we're continuing to pay someone who literally sleeps on the job. How's she going to watch two?"

"It's dangerous to extrapolate," I said. I thought about Babette's husband looking for work. "Maybe this only happened a few times." I worried this was tacit encouragement for further espionage.

"Once is enough." Sarah sat back. "Once is unacceptable."

Moses leapt onto the couch and curled up in her lap.

"We can't be rash." I bounced my foot. "Babette is a huge part of Sophie's life—our life."

"She's an employee, babe. We pay her to do a job, an extremely important one at that. It's clear that Sophie has seen her do this before, enough to repeat Babette's excuse."

Sarah brought her fingers to her lips. I rubbed her shoulder, feeling more of my own tension. "I know it's not right. But just think for a second—they're safe inside the apartment. The place is still babyproofed."

Sarah shrugged out from under my hand; Moses seemed to balk too. "What if Sophie was choking? I can't believe I'm having to convince you."

"Imagine it was an afternoon when Sophie was with your mom, and she happened to nod off briefly on the couch? Babette woke right up when Sophie came over."

"My mom's not a narcoleptic."

"Babette is family," I said.

Sarah looked surprised. "I know this sounds cold, but let's be honest: the whole *nanny as part of the family* thing is the bullshit we tell ourselves to feel better. *Sophie* is family. We should've known this with Babette's age."

Sarah had picked up enough speed to bypass my hesitation.

"So, what do you think we should do?" I asked. "We can't just cut her loose. That's ruthless."

"Why do you keep thinking of this from her perspective?"

"I'm thinking about this from Sophie's perspective. It's a lot to ask of her to get used to another nanny."

"You need to consider us—which will be the four of us soon. *We're* your family."

After lunch the next day, I sat in a meeting that ran for over two hours, glad to focus on something that wasn't Babette's narcolepsy. But when I returned to my office, I found another email from Sarah. No subject line. I opened it and saw two clips, both of which were dated earlier in the day. *Too big to text*, it read above the first. *Volume up*, below the second. I felt trapped by Sarah's insistence.

The first clip opened with Babette, again, stretched out on the couch. My stomach tightened and I closed the clip. The other clip showed Babette and Grace, a nanny in our building who watched a boy Sophie's age. They had playdates frequently. The four of them sat in the living room; I turned up the volume. Sophie was singing "Following the Leader," ignoring Mikey, the little boy. When this stopped, they played with magnet tiles on the floor, and I could hear the stray clacking plastic. Then I heard the adult voices. Grace was younger than Babette, strident as she spoke. *You need to ask them for a raise*, she said. *These people are rich, it's nothing to them. Don't let them take advantage of you.* Grace went on to tell Babette how she had demanded more money at her last year-end review. She told Babette that, honestly, she needed to talk to me. Babette's laughter was startling. *Please*, she said. *You know that man is scared for his life in here. He's a punk. I'd have better luck asking the cat for more money.*

I tensed. My legs locked up. I looked over my shoulder like I was the one being watched. I played the clip once more to hear her self-satisfied laughter, to see her frail old body jiggle. Then I slammed the laptop shut.

When I got home that night, Moses's feeder had been moved to the other side of the room, positioned with a clearer view of the couch.

"Hey, Jordan," Babette said.

I dropped my bag to the floor; I mustered a *hey*.

Sarah glared at me before she spoke. "Did you just call him Jordan, Babette?"

Babette turned back and forth between us, as if she thought we were playing a joke on her. Sophie colored furiously at the table as the three of us stood in silence. Then Babette's face opened up; she palmed her mouth and her eyes dilated. "I'm so sorry."

I feigned a smile without speaking, then nodded.

"Gosh—I'm embarrassed."

"What you guys talkinabout?" Sophie perked up. This was something she'd started asking lately, whenever adults spoke in nontoddler-inflected voices.

Sarah stroked Sophie's hair and said it was nothing. Moses's head reared up from the couch.

Babette came over to me. "Jordan was my old boss. I worked for them for so many years."

Then she reached out for a hug, her body soft against mine.

"I hope you're not offended. I must be getting old!"

Sarah leaned her head, pretending to doze off behind her.

"It happens," I said.

After Babette packed up to leave, I walked her to the door. She spoke before I could. "Did you hear back?"

I was confused. "About what?"

"The job for my husband?"

I couldn't believe her gall. "I've only started asking about it. I need more time."

"I really appreciate what you're doing for us, so thank you."

"Listen," I started. "Sarah and I are hoping to talk to you on Friday. Just for a few minutes after work?"

"Of course," she said. Her face stiffened for a moment as she pulled her glasses out of her bag. "I'm really sorry I called you

Jordan," she said. I could see under the light that her lenses were slicked with grime.

The next evening, Sarah skipped Sophie's bath and got her down early. I waited for her in the living room with a glass of seltzer, avoiding alcohol's dulling effect. Sarah poured herself a sip of the Orvieto we'd brought back from Umbria the previous summer.

"You still in a *mood*?" she asked.

"Just thinking about Babette."

"I feel like maybe I was a little rash before," she said. "I was getting sentimental thinking about how sweet she was with Sophie as a newborn. The way she was with her bottle. We were lucky to find her when we did."

I was surprised by her soft turn. "I know," I said. "But I was thinking about what you said about the family before."

"Oh?" Moses sat still beside her feet. "So you think she's got to go?"

I stopped short of an about-face. "The prospect of hiring someone new is daunting. I've been torn," I said. "But clearly now Babette's naps are a pattern."

"I knew the nannies talked behind our backs, but that clip was excessive."

I nodded in agreement. "And look," I said, pointing to a small stain on the carpet. "Babette used to clean stuff like this. She's letting a lot slip."

Sarah pursed her lips at me. "My mom offered to help us out if we needed it. She thinks we should let her go too."

Tired of water, I got up to pour myself wine. "So, how do we do this? We're supposed to tell Babette we've been surveilling her?"

"In the state of New York, it's entirely legal to have a camera installed on your property for protection."

I pictured Sarah, hunched over her laptop, devouring the stipulations of law.

"Sophie brought it to our attention, anyway," she said. "We don't have a nanny cam, technically. We've never monitored Babette before. It's only by chance that we found this out."

"I suppose we're simply confirming something that Sophie told us," I said. The wine caused a band of heat to form in the middle of my face. "I already told Babette we needed to speak to her on Friday."

Sarah set her glass down and inched closer to me. "Wow, babe," she said. Her energy shifted suddenly. She looked at her phone and clicked something closed before tossing it onto the couch. Then she shooed Moses away with her foot.

She mounted me. I stared at her mouth. She kissed me hard and bit my lip. Gripping my throat, she rose over me. We had fucked in the living room after finding out she was pregnant again, which before then we hadn't done in months. As she started sucking my neck, I noticed the glossy white cat feeder in the corner of the room, with its tiny light on.

When Friday arrived, I felt nervous. I'd never fired anyone; we had scripted talking points.

Sophie buried her face in her alligator stuffie in the living room. "My love, what are you doing?" I asked her.

"She's been silly all day, this one. I tell you." Babette wore her burgundy Juicy hoodie with rhinestones, the one her husband had gotten her last Christmas. She sat in the chair beside me.

Sarah hovered in the kitchen, making herself tea.

"So, what did you guys get up to today?" she asked. She eyed me as she dipped her tea bag.

"Aw, we had a lot of fun, huh, Soph?" Babette pitched her head as she spoke. "We drew. We played restaurant. We went to the playground with Grace and Mikey."

Sarah sat in one of the chairs facing us.

"Sophie climbed the big ladder all by herself. Even Mikey's still too scared!" Babette chuckled.

Sophie looked up. "He's *scared*." She bared her tiny teeth at me.

"Thanks for making some time to talk with us," I said. "Firstly, we want to thank you for how wonderful you've been with Sophie. I don't think we tell you that enough. From the first time we met you, you never stopped teaching us how to be parents."

Sarah widened her eyes at me. Babette mumbled some appreciation; her hands lay cupped in her lap.

"And we know just how exhausting the work can be," Sarah interjected.

I stared back at her. "We've been thinking a lot about Sophie and how the next few years will play out, preparing to start preschool, deciding what her schedule will be like."

Babette nodded along.

"A lot is changing," I said. "And we feel like we too need to make a change."

I could only look at Babette for another second. Instead, I focused on a new, small stain on the Moroccan rug. A dry discoloration camouflaged by the spiral pattern near her feet.

"What you guys talkinabout?" Sophie had clued in to the room's changing tenor. Her face was blank, innocent.

Sarah got up and grabbed Sophie to sit on her lap.

"Our childcare needs have evolved, Babette," I continued. "And we're really sorry, but we're going to have to let you go."

She looked down, hanging her head. Then she looked over at Sophie. "What?" she said finally. "I'm shocked. I didn't think it was this— I thought I was getting a raise!"

"We're giving you a month's severance, and we'll write a good review for you on the Tribeca Nannies site. You'll find another family to work with," I assured her.

"It's not even been three years." Babette's eyes filled with tears. "You said how much finding someone for the long term was important to you all when I first interviewed. Someone to grow with Sophie. I was so sure I would be with you all for ten years at least. I love Sophie so much. I can't bear to think about leaving her."

Babette looked for Sophie again, but she was resting against Sarah's shoulder. Sarah kissed the top of Sophie's head.

"I know this is hard," I said. "It's been such a tough decision for us too."

"Tell me—why are you firing me? What have I done? I've only ever been good to you."

Babette's voice grew loud. Moses darted across the carpet, startling me.

"Sophie needs more active engagement, someone who's able to scrabble around on the floor with her."

"But you knew that wasn't me when you hired me. And I *do* play with her, entertain her, all the time. I never misled you."

I lowered my voice a bit. "Sophie said you were sleeping during the day."

"What?" Babette looked indignant. "I only ever rest my head when she naps. I never sleep!" She paused momentarily and raised her fist to her mouth. "I thought you were decent people. But I'm a fool."

I stood up and glanced at the cat feeder. Moses feasted from it now. "Babette, you don't even clean anymore," I said. "We come home to dirty dishes."

"Now you're really lying," Babette yelled.

"Look." I pointed at the stains on the rug. "Why are there stains?" I was angry now. "That's unacceptable."

Sophie started to cry, sniffling. She covered her face. Sarah rose and took Sophie down the hall to her room.

"This isn't you," Babette said quietly. "She's putting you up to it."

"It *is* me, Babette," I said. "*I'm* firing you."

She started to weep. I sat with her for a minute as she gathered herself, then led her to the door. Her sobs echoed in the empty hall as I shut the door behind her.

On Monday morning, when I left the bathroom after showering, Moses loped down the hallway and clawed my toes. I splayed myself against the wall, failing to deter him by flicking water from my feet. I ran away and finally closed him off from my room to get dressed for work.

"Are you starting to feel relieved?" Sarah asked when I came into the kitchen. "I'm proud when I think about how you handled it. We did the right thing, babe." She pinched some sea salt onto my overnight oats and fed me the first bite. "I've already found a woman I love," she said. "Early education degree. Young. Vibrant. Well rested."

Sarah's mom was heading into town soon to help for a bit. I wished my mom could do the same, and I realized then that Babette would never drive me to basketball again. In truth, I was wary of another nanny—the way a new person in the house inevitably reveals and refracts new aspects of yourself.

"She's coming on Wednesday to meet us," Sarah said. She came close to me. "Today's going to be a good day," she said. "I can feel it."

After a strategy meeting later that day, I returned to my office to find an email from Sarah. The subject line: XoX. I turned away from the screen, incredulous. The sole relief of the last days was not having to confront another one of these videos; it was gratuitous at this point. I almost didn't open it. But when I looked again, I saw that the clip was dark—nighttime—and the view of our living room was dim. After I pressed play, it took a minute to distinguish the large form on the couch as two people. I watched the bright points of my eyes peering back at me. Sarah and I were having sex.

I got up to close my office door. When I came back to resume the clip, Sarah moved slowly on top of me as I reached into her hair. My face flushed before my computer screen to witness it; I'd never seen myself in this way, in the motion of fucking. The clip was just over twelve minutes. I scrolled ahead, impatient, our positions staggering and changing. Toward the end, Sarah had come to sit behind me. She held a hand roughly over my mouth as she reached around. My lips now were dry while I watched her stroking me, watched her muffling my moans as she finished me off. The clip stopped abruptly. I sat back in my chair and stared at the final frame. I remembered this moment, just before I'd gone to the kitchen to get a towel. Right before I'd crouched down on my bare knees and tried to scrub clean the stain I'd left on the rug.

PIZZA PARTY

Tom hasn't made pizza from scratch in at least three years. His daughter, Evelyn, is coming over for dinner with her new fiancé, so he must tonight. A margherita pie, one with pickled peppers and trumpet mushrooms, and a hot honey and pepperoni situation. His pizza has been her favorite food since she was four.

It shouldn't matter that he hasn't seen her in six months. He and Evelyn have always had a mature relationship, one that began with Tom's determination never to speak to her in that pandering, childlike voice most parents used. It wasn't until after the divorce that he understood her maturity. At twelve, she'd palmed both of her ears when they sat her down. *I'm not getting in the middle. I want a relationship with you both*, she'd said.

He pours himself a glass of the Chianti he'd purchased at a roadside vendor in Tuscany last year. The perfect prologue to cooking, he thinks. His home is ready: Early afternoon light filters through a skylight into the large deVOL Shaker kitchen he'd designed. The dining table pine scented and dust free.

He turns Debussy's *Images II* on the stereo and sets out his steel mixing bowls. His movements are practiced, if hesitant. Yes, time has passed since he's gotten his hands dirty, but he's made dough hundreds of times before. In the days following Evelyn's birth, he and Kylie had ample empty hours in the warmth of their two-bedroom D.C. apartment in which he nurtured a new interest in pizza. The salad days before he'd opened his first restaurant, before he'd gone to Naples to get certified by a weathered pizzaiolo, before his wife had fucked his restaurant partner and he'd subsequently sold the business. The days when he'd make pies at home between Evelyn's naps and feedings and the park walks with her strapped to his chest. Each time brought a new sense of accomplishment. He was pretty sure he and Kylie had been happiest then. If nothing else, those months were the simplest of his life.

A small basil plant sits in its Noguchi planter and Tom guides it along the counter, to the center of the sunlight. It was a gift from a recent trip to an urban nursery. Usually these visits with potential business partners—especially sustainability-forward ones—left him energized, but this trip he'd felt overwhelmed walking through the brief rows of herbs, the tiny shoots reaching so eagerly skyward.

He tears a green leaf from the plant and grinds it between his teeth. The scent is lemony and peppery and slightly sweet. Evelyn had hated basil when she was little. Addressing waiters at his restaurant, she'd strike a finger in the air and announce, "But *no* basil," until she no longer had to order at all. (The Evelyn, as the plain pizza became known as on the menu.)

Limey bubbles of cold-pressed olive oil disperse in the warm water. He pours the yeast over top, and it forms a sandy lid before slowly fizzing and dissolving. He grabs his iPhone as he waits for a murky liquid to form—murky liquid, he thinks, like that from whence his ex-wife came. She'd texted him that morning to remind him to be *welcoming* to Bryce, Evelyn's fiancé. He was a former debater, like Evelyn, and she really seemed to like him. Tom feels a pang of something—not the typical indignation at Kylie's directives, but maybe fear that Evelyn will be the one to cancel, like she had for Easter dinner. He'd messaged her last night, confirming the time. She'd offered to bring the coffee-soaked gingersnap dessert he'd taught her to make at his apartment in Philadelphia, shortly after he moved. But Tom said he had everything covered, which reminded him that he'd forgotten to buy ice cream. A trip to the store would cut into his time, which was now under three hours.

He swigs his wine and sets it down on the butcher-block kitchen island. The centerpiece—his station. He's had the island for over a decade, one of the first pieces he'd bought for himself when he got a place of his own. It has moved with him from several apartments and houses. It is the one surface upon which he allows disorder. There's character in the wood's many scratches, grooves, and cuts: his own history, more importantly, a network of scuffs to be imprinted on the meal.

He starts to mix the dough, making a hollow in the double-zero flour and pouring the yeasty liquid carefully into the center. He'll use his hands to mix it, which is purer and more ancient, instead of using the stand mixer. Despite the mess, he relishes scraping away the crust from his fingers once it's dry, like shedding a skin.

He begins kneading and turning the dough for several minutes until the huge pale lump is smooth. He slaps and thuds the dough onto the wood, his shoulders aching from the pressure. (He no longer exercises, so these discrete bits of exertion are humbling.) His appetite for dining, the accompanying ceremony of it, has always been greater than his appetite for food, which keeps him in size 30/34 slacks, and perhaps makes him an ideal restaurateur. He's been considering slowing down with work lately, or at least being more silent in his future partnerships. His last restaurant venture—at a boutique hotel restaurant in Dubrovnik—had been a resounding success; but it had taxed him. A fire four weeks before its opening had portended catastrophe, which they'd narrowly avoided. As a result he'd missed Evelyn's high school graduation to stay behind and deal with it. To redeem himself, he'd chartered a boat for her and three friends off the Dalmatian coast as a graduation gift, with several nights in the hotel's premier suite. She'd claimed her clothing smelled like smoke for weeks after she'd returned home, but he'd seen the pictures—the shards of sun on the water, the large sunglasses and translucent rosé—and knew she'd covet the memories.

After an hour, he removes the large dough ball and sets it on the butcher block. He pats it gently several times. There's something mammalian about it, like a disembodied stomach. He pictures himself then, alone on a remote beach in too-short, too-bright swim trunks rubbing suntan oil onto his small belly.

He cuts the dough neatly into quarters to form the individual pies. He rolls them carefully into rounds along the wood, douses four bowls with olive oil, and covers them with plastic lids. This rise is the longest and most important. Ideally, he'd let it rise for four hours—to get that slightly sour, hyperpuffy dough—but he is already running behind, having misjudged the amount of flour in the jar because it had stuck high to the glass in the pantry. Two hours is all he can afford.

Before he leaves for the store, he prepares the sauce: San Marzano tomatoes with olive oil, honey, garlic, cayenne, and a dash of fresh oregano. It takes just six seconds to blend, and he empties it into a Ball jar to cool and thicken in the fridge.

The grocery store is freezing. The sudden change in temperature is jarring. The cold rises along Tom's arms and neck and diffuses into a dizziness behind his eyes.

In the frozen foods aisle, he faces a grid of pints. He can't decide between the Häagen-Dazs vanilla (which he'd used at his restaurants before they made ice cream from scratch), and something small batch and fancier. He feels a hand on his shoulder.

"This guy," Travis says. "I never see you anymore."

Tom feigns a welcome surprise, baring his teeth. They hug tentatively. "I've been away," he says. "Things have been unexpectedly busy of late."

"So I hear," Travis says. "Congratulations are in order."

"You're far too kind," Tom says. "I really never expected Dubrovnik to take off in the way it did. We're doing another in Split. And there's interest in Zadar. A Balkan empire."

Travis looks bemused. "I mean Evie," he says.

"Oh," Tom says. He hates when others insist on calling her Evie. "Of course, of course. They're actually coming over for dinner tonight, to celebrate."

"You must be thrilled," Travis says.

"She's too young for marriage, if I'm honest." Tom reaches his hand out to grab the freezer's door handle awkwardly. He pretends to scrutinize the flavors for a minute. "Enough about me— How're things? How's Lena these days?"

Lena and Evelyn had been close friends in middle school.

"Actually, she transferred to the hospitality program at Cornell," Travis says. "I may be calling you for guidance."

"Have her email me," Tom says. "I'd be happy to pull strings."

At home, he pours himself another glass of wine and peeks through the lids of the bowls, set out evenly on the island. None of them have risen much. No condensation has formed, no bubbles in the dough. When he'd first started teaching Evelyn to make pizza—she was a little girl—this had been her favorite part. To watch the surface of the dough rife with bubbles, otherworldly and alive, made young Evelyn conjure magic. He wants to remember what it felt like to teach her, to show her something novel again.

It's nearing three o'clock: only two hours remain before she arrives. He decides to shower. In the mirror upstairs, he studies his salt-and-pepper part. He'd gotten his hair cut yesterday—five inches on the sides and three on top—which he always did right before seeing Evelyn after a stretch, as if to disprove that so much time had passed. He removes his glasses and pokes the coves of shadow under his eyes, pulling gently at the skin. No one knows he uses concealer, but on occasion he forgets to rub it in after applying and gives himself away. This would be a mortifying mistake tonight, he thinks, though in some way maybe it would be endearing to Evelyn.

He lets the water run and shuts the door to seal the room with steam. He'll do some breathing exercises to calm himself, the ones his therapist forced him to try and that he has learned not to hate.

He goes to the spare room. Everything is in its right place—the Matouk duvet he'd imported and the new nightstand. It feels slightly empty apart from this, or maybe just decorated enough to entice her imagination (he'd ordered some La Prairie skin care products from Switzerland earlier in the week to put on the shelf). It's not a blank canvas, quite, but a blank page in a coloring book.

In the room's small closet, he grabs a towel (also Matouk) from the backup storage shelf. At his feet is a frame turned toward the wall, one that he'd forgotten about. He still hasn't shown Evelyn. She'd always wanted to go to Japan; he'd found the vintage print called *Tomatoes at Mt. Fuji*, a bright silk screen. The poster contains aspects of them both, he'd thought at the time. He considers putting it up before Evelyn arrives, but it will look strange as the only piece mounted on the wall.

Tom has always assumed that Evelyn understood the pain from the divorce was enough to justify his moving away. All the travel and commitment to work—she enjoyed his success.

Everyone had gossiped about the affair, and he felt emasculated by the shame. But he'd been back in D.C. for two years now, to be closer to Evelyn, and she'd yet to spend a night at his place.

He steps into the bathroom's dense warmth. The steam moves in thick whorls. He is enveloped by it, and struck by a memory: A French chef had told him once about his method of proofing his sourdough in the bathroom, the way the temperature and moisture helped expedite the process. He'd always thought it sounded dubious, or insane, but now, he feels, it can't hurt.

He runs downstairs and grabs the bowls. It takes two trips. He sets three on the vanity and the last on the floor. Every few minutes, he peeks from the shower at the fogged lids. He feels crazed. But order, sometimes, is only maintained by a spontaneous risk like this.

Another hour down, and only one left. Back at the island, he begins opening the lids, and his heart falls; the tightly compact balls show no signs of rising. They might as well have been Play-Doh.

He starts pressing and stretching the dough into flat rounds. The second one tears as soon as he pulls it. He curses under his breath and slams his fist against the island's wood. With the music no longer playing, the sound is loud. He ignores the pain. He re-rolls the dough and flattens it again; it is now an unkempt mass that he vows to use only as a last resort.

He covers each round with a tea towel. The island is neat again, all mistakes draped and concealed by linen. He remembers a time, early on at his first restaurant, when the thermostat had been accidentally set to Celsius. They'd had to make an entire new batch of dough with only hours to spare before they opened the next day. Crucially, they'd pulled it off.

He sets the oven to 500 degrees. While he waits, he mixes the arugula, fresh croutons, and pickled radishes for the salad, pouring the vinaigrette he'd made last night into a small carafe. Then he sets the table, laying out three place settings—which look sad in their asymmetry. He arranges an extra and fetches two new candles to put in the candelabra. He turns the music on again and dims the light to 30 percent.

When the oven's thermostat rings, he gets the tomato sauce and mozzarella from the fridge and puts everything out on the butcher block. The toppings sit neatly in their bowls. He uncovers the dough, begins to dress the pies, spiraling his tomato-sauce-drenched spoon clockwise around the dough and leaving about three-quarters of an inch of crust to help mask any imperfection. He imagines Evelyn's fiancé, his face cinched in confusion by the uninspired pizza being served by a man whose pedigree precedes him.

Five o'clock: two pies cook on the oven's middle rack. Not terrible, he thinks. He takes a second to focus on his breathing. He presses his middle fingers gently against his thumbs. He tries not to peek inside the oven, knowing that a watched pie bakes, if not never, then excruciatingly slowly. But he can't help it. The cheese bubbles, the red sauce is starting to shimmer. Still, the crust looks stale—like a thick cracker. He'll put it under the broiler if necessary, singe and burn it as a last resort.

The doorbell rings then; he nearly falls back. "One sec," he yells out. Evelyn's never early. He wipes his hands on a dish towel and walks to the door.

A short UPS woman stands before him, with red hair and dark eyeliner.

Relief rushes over him.

She offers him a small brown box with modern branding. The La Prairie products for Evelyn. The woman eyes his shoulder then, a dish towel slung over it. She leans her head forward slightly. "Smells good."

He signs her device with a finger, thanking her.

"Pizza?" She looks behind him toward the kitchen.

"You're good," he says. His food smells the part, at least.

"My husband bought a portable pizza oven," she says. "He's obsessed—all *biga* this, *biga* that."

He holds the doorknob, trying earnestly to listen to her.

"My kids love it."

He remembers cutting Evelyn's pizza up into tiny squares when she used to eat in a high chair, the way she'd held a piece up like the tiny tile of a game she had no idea how to play.

The woman looks back at her truck, its lights flashing in the drive. "Buon appetito," she says.

He sets the box down by the door and rushes back to the oven. Crouching, he eyes the pizza through the oven window. The heat blanches his face through the glass. The mozzarella has browned in spots, more scorched than is appropriate. He opens the oven and grabs his metal pizza peel from the counter. Guiding it in, he tries to fit both pies onto it to remove them quickly. One falls facefirst on the open oven door's window. He flinches. "Fuck!" he yells. As he tries to save it, the peel smacks against the rack and the second pizza slides to the peel's edge. He steps back to level it, which only causes the pie to fall to the floor. For a second he doesn't move. Two down. The heat from the oven reaches his knees, creeping up to his stomach. Streaks of grease from the mozzarella gleam on the floor. He shuts his eyes. The hairs on his arms stand on end. He kneels and tries to salvage the floor pie, sweeping hot cheese back into the center. Two of his fine white hairs, almost like highlights, appear in the tomato.

He rises then. He begins to shake. A second later he pushes the oven door shut with his foot. The pizza inside falls back, leaving a massacre of red sauce on the window.

On the butcher-block island, two rounds of dough remain. One is shitty, yes, but if united, they might bake into one large, capable crust. If the dough is pressed flat enough, and spread wide enough, he might salvage the meal.

He deals with the mess on the floor first. Once it is clean, he rinses his hands, and then he's back at the island mashing dough. He wipes the sweat from his forehead with his arm. He folds the dough in on itself several times to strengthen it before flattening. His hands won't do, he realizes. He finds his large wooden rolling pin, one he hasn't used in months. It's covered in a thin layer of sticky dust. He scrubs it quickly in the sink, wipes it dry with a towel.

He rolls the dough into an oblong shape. As he attempts to pull it into a loose rectangle, the dough begins again to tear in opposing corners. He notices several additional holes forming in the middle as well. A tiny, agonized face with a gaping mouth. He tries one last time to roll the pin across and repair the damage. This only makes things worse. He squeezes the pin's handle and lifts it high. When it crashes against the island a pain shoots through his wrist. The satisfaction of the act prevails. He repeatedly whacks the thin dough, the stupid little face that has formed in it. Gashes strafe the surface. He imagines Bryce concealing judgment behind a dumb grin, imagines the postmortem he and Evelyn will have as soon as they leave his place. They were never going to stay the night, were they?

He beats the pin against the butcher block's edge as hard as he can. Again and again, almost in rhythm. Soon, a chunk of wood cracks from it. Sweat is forming, heat reaching his neck and creeping around his ears. The pin slips out of his hand, and he begins hitting his chest, a stray fist knocking his forehead. It's like there is some sleeping creature trapped inside of himself that he's trying to awaken.

Once he stops, he wipes his eyes. How quickly and stupidly it has all come undone. And he's supposed to be a pro. A renewed anger rises in him. He scrapes the dough free from the island in pieces, feels it gathering under his nails. He flings chunks against the wall. Had the dough risen properly it would've stuck to the surface next to his Chagall lithograph, but instead it simply falls to the floor. His breathing is heavy; he feels sick. Or hungry. Save for the wine earlier, his stomach is empty.

He stares at the unused scraps. He is starved, and for a moment he considers tasting his mess. He tenses his gut, imagines himself retching. *I'm sick*, he thinks. *Sick*. The realization brings a wave of relief as if he's just vomited.

He grabs his phone and pulls up Evelyn's last message. He stares at her name; if she only knew all that he had done. The words come easy. Food poisoning, irrefutable. Before sending it, he wonders what she's doing. Changing her outfit? One last look in the mirror? They have no car, but he pictures Bryce behind the wheel of one. Waiting outside for her, the posture of any patient fiancé. A honking horn blares in Tom's head. He hopes they haven't left already and won't be forced to turn around.

Before he's able to hit send, the doorbell rings. He can't bring himself to get up. Maybe if he stays quiet enough, they will leave. He listens. After another minute, he hears the keys. He'd forgotten that he'd given one to Evelyn.

"Dad?"

He rises. He wipes his hands on his pants.

"Are you here?"

He walks past the oven and feels the change in temperature. "I'm here," he says.

Evelyn's long golden hair has been curled. She looks much older with the small A.P.C. clutch he'd gotten her hanging from her shoulder. She's holding wine. Bryce is tall, taller than Tom by several inches. His own tawny head is too small for his body.

Tom shakes his hand. "I'm glad you could come," he says.

"Whoa," Bryce says. "This place is unreal."

"Dad, are you sick?" Evelyn says. "What's going on?"

Tom gives her a hug. He wants to hang his head on her shoulder. "Just a small kitchen malfunction. You didn't have to bring wine." He takes the bottle from her and they walk toward the kitchen. His mess is visible on the floor, the dough scraps and rolling pin. To Tom it looks, in the moment, like a giant's toothpick and the food he'd removed from his enormous teeth.

"What happened?" she asks. "You never leave a mess."

He looks at the sauce streaked on the oven's glass. "The pizza didn't go to plan."

She scrunches her face and looks at him more closely. "Don't worry," she says. Her posture slackens, and she leans in. "It's fine."

"No, it's not."

"What smells so good?" Bryce says.

Tom realizes it's the salad dressing, the shallots and garlic pungent. "There's a consolation salad."

"I love salad," Bryce says.

Evelyn smiles at Tom, rubbing his upper arm. "Yeah, me too."

"Let's have a drink," Tom says. "I'll open the bottle you sweetly brought."

He grabs the corkscrew— It's a fifteen-dollar Malbec, he thinks. But then he thinks, That's fine.

They sit down at the table. Bryce can't help but look around the apartment. His eyes widen as he sees the sound system's tall teak speakers. He looks, to Tom, like a tourist who's just gotten his room upgraded to a suite.

Tom feels that the boy is naïve, but that maybe the other parts of him satisfy Evelyn. Tom sits up. "Let's order a couple of pies."

Evelyn stares at him. "Wait, are you serious?"

Tom grins.

"I don't think I've ever heard you say that," she says.

After years of eschewing delivery in even the most unsuitable situations, like Evelyn's eighth birthday party, with all those tiny dirty fingers poking his dough, he realizes, now, that it will have to be enough.

They all raise their glasses. Tom presses his tongue against the roof of his mouth as he tastes the cheap wine—like a diluted juice—and he smiles despite this. To swallow it is disgusting.

DEPENDENTS

Sixty-two years and change, and I finally get why they warn you about pride. I'm flat, can barely move the lower half of my body, which is completely exposed. Naked save a crisp dress shirt, wrists bound by my father's ebony cuff links. My thighs sweat beneath a pillow covering my crotch. I'd managed to pull myself up onto the bed from the floor after a struggle, so at least I'm assed out in a hotel and not my house; makes everything seem a little less permanent. I have several more hours before I'm needed to welcome guests. For a moment, while I'm motionless, it feels like there hasn't been any pain at all.

This is how the injury happened: I'd tried to put my boxers on while standing up, attempting to lasso my stray foot with the elastic band. When I stepped through, I missed, shifted my weight, and felt a violent spasm in my hips before hitting the floor. Throwing my back out might've been a routine setback, but I'd had a minor stroke two months before, while washing my car. As I was wiping the cloth across the door, the warped sun spots against the metal made me dizzy and I struggled to stand. I went inside to get water, and Teresa knew something was off, told me to sit. I'm fine, I said. I remember the sound of the plastic bucket cracking beneath the tire as we sped from the driveway.

I'd only lost partial feeling in my right leg, and it was a chore to speak clearly at first, though I overcame about 80 percent of the limp-lipped sensation after a few weeks. I did two weeks of rehab at the hospital, then Teresa drove me to a specialized facility where I spent hours each day trying to rebuild the mind-body connection. I swam. I dropped twenty pounds. I stopped smoking and drinking (half a pilsner at dinner and my symptoms crept back). But I had good reason to turn my life around in such short order: my daughter Lisa was getting married. I told the two nurses at the rehab clinic that I wanted to be the one to walk her down the aisle, that I needed to give my speech on sturdy legs. They took the task more seriously than I did.

From the bed, I see my speech—folded sheets of paper on the mahogany desk. I should've memorized it by now (I didn't want to be the type to refer to a paper). But I hadn't been able to look it over without weeping. Not even a bit. The first sentence was like a gash and the speech's entire sentiment leaked from it. My doctor had mentioned the dormant chambers of the brain that could awaken after a stroke, but I wasn't ready at all for what I'd felt.

Lisa is technically my stepdaughter, though her mom hates when I say that. I'd legally adopted her when she was fifteen, and she's called me Dad for years. Her father was a coked-out chef and not involved despite his best efforts at sobriety. My ex-wife might say I was also an absent father. Garrett, my birth son, is five years older than Lisa. There's some tension between the two, but they pretend to get along, and Garrett's in town for the wedding. Finding us all together was rare, and now it had been twice, on account of my stroke. My masterstroke, I'd joked, when the hospital room in Westchester was full of family.

Half an hour ago, I'd been ready to stand, walk, and even dance a glacial waltz with Lisa. Now I require an extra set of hands to get my fucking underwear on. I know I need Garrett to help me. It's the only way. And for the last week, as it became clear I couldn't handle the task of reading the speech, I'd planned to ask him to do it for me. He has a great voice, and I could stand next to him trying to keep my shit together. Putting my pants on is the first step of making any of this happen.

My forehead is tight from the dried sweat, the phone warm against my ear. As I shift my weight, pain courses through my hips and into my lower back. I want to crawl under the covers.

"Dad—what's up?"

He sounds surprised.

"How was the trip?" I ask.

"A delay outside Wilmington but mostly good. How's the father of the bride?"

I can sense his cheeky smile (he can think whatever he wants about Lisa and me).

"I saw that video of you doing lunges," he continues. "Looking good."

"Listen, can you come by my room?"

"Now?"

"Not urgent, just need a favor."

"Actually," Garrett says, "there's something I wanted to talk to you about anyway."

I ask him to grab me a spare room key from the concierge and a bottle of Advil while he's out. He's running an errand for his girlfriend, the most recent of half a dozen or so who I'd met, and she seems uniquely skeptical of me. Who knows what Garrett has told her. He was only nine when his mother and I divorced. I'd wanted to stick around Philly, but I got a big job at a real estate firm in New York soon after. I'd taken Garrett to the Japanese steak house where we sat on the floor and ate in socks, hoping to soften the news I was about to tell him—that I was moving. His mother had allowed him to get a buzz cut in what seemed like an act of protest against the divorce. He didn't order his typical second Shirley Temple and barely ate a bite of his steak teriyaki.

I try to lean up on an elbow, and even that hurts. I chuckle to myself, as if acknowledging how pathetic I feel will help lessen it. I think it's some feat that this degree of helplessness is rare to me, that perhaps I'd done some things right in life for that to be the case. Despite this, I'm not sure how best to avoid appearing to Garrett like a belly-up dog or a preshoot porn star. God, the pallor of my thighs.

My next thought is that Garrett needs money. Typically, this is why he calls or says he wants to talk. The excitement of seeing his name on my phone gives way to the fact that he is, though a grown man, very much still a dependent. But I'd gladly cut a check for his help right now. The return on investment in this case would be fruitful, in the way his gym franchise idea wasn't. He can help me triage my capabilities. The father-daughter dance is out of the question, but I should be able to stand upright. Pop six Advil and maybe even walk Lisa down the aisle.

I think of Garrett's face the first time he heard Lisa call me Dad. Disbelief followed by a wry, self-satisfied judgment. The shit. We'd never discussed it. But I loved Lisa, loved how I was with her. It's almost like I got to watch myself be an ideal parent, acting the part. A kind of Method fathering.

I'm close to dozing, but I hear a knock at the door. Quickly I adjust my groin pillow.

"It's Garrett," he says, muffled.

"Use the key."

He enters slowly. I hear the hallway's faint din, the door latching shut behind him. After a minute he peeks his head around the corner. His blond hair is starting to go sandy, the grays coming in, which I hadn't noticed the last time I saw him. He's gained a few, I can see, despite the baggy hoodie. Everyone had always expected him to be as tall as I am, but he'd never had the spurt.

He eyes my dark plaid boxers on the floor. "Did you shit yourself?"

I laugh. "I threw my back out."

"Jesus," he says. He places the plastic bag on the desk. He doesn't know where to stand.

"I'll be fine," I say. "Get me a Diet Coke from the mini fridge. The Advil."

He brings me the slim silver can and pills. "You gonna be all right for tonight?"

"I've got some time, thank God." With the pills, I drink nearly the entire soda before setting it down on the side table. The pillow slips, and Garrett turns away. "We're both men," I say. "Just help me get my fucking boxers on."

"Are you serious?"

"Serious as a stroke."

He starts to speak but stops, looking at the boxers on the floor. Then he looks back to the bed, like he's trying to figure out how to accommodate a sofa delivery.

"Seems like a job for Teresa to me?"

"I haven't told Teresa yet. She's off getting her hair done with Lisa. I don't want to worry them. The last thing Lisa needs today."

Finally, he bends and pinches my boxers to lift them.

"They're clean, you asshole," I say.

We briefly discuss how this is going to happen. I attempt to lift my legs so Garrett can slide the boxers up, but I lack the core strength. The pain is too much. He comes to my side and locks his arm into mine to help me sit. His scent is cheap, like Irish Spring, and I remember the way I used to lather up his thick blond hair in the bath. He arranges a stack of pillows for me to rest on. I take a deep breath.

"Step one," I say. The change makes a dampness in my butt-crack apparent.

"I'm gonna turn you a bit," he says. "Try and lean closer to the edge."

I keep the pillow pressed firmly into my lap and lean my weight in his direction. When he slips his palm under my calves, one at a time, my balls shrink. It has been two months, apart from the ninety-second episode with Teresa last week, since I've been touched intimately.

Garrett's face is focused on his hands, as if he's defusing a bomb, as if the explosion he's trying to prevent is my nudity. I stare at the discolored edge of his incisor as he opens his mouth.

"OK," he says. "How's that?"

The pain is minimal. I take another deep breath. My feet are dangling from the bed.

Garrett steps back.

"Just put them over my ankles," I say. "I'll take it from there."

"You shouldn't strain yourself," he says.

His sudden concern is conspicuous, like he's baiting me. I say I'm fine.

"How much did this wedding set you back anyway? You never told me."

Whether he's enjoying the spectacle of my current state or simply amused at the situation, I'm unsure. The wedding cost $125,000, which is just a hair less than I feared. I clench my ass, up through my dick, and squeeze the pillow. I can almost reach the boxers with a toe, and it's a torment. "Garrett, stop fucking around," I say. I feel more sweat gathering under my arms.

Finally he relents, kneels down. He loops the boxers around my ankles and pulls them up to my knees. I worry that I smell, though I'd showered recently. I refuse to indulge the thought that I will inevitably arrive at a place of such abased reliance, that it's only a matter of time.

I pull at the waistband, alternating at either side with my right hand. That Garrett simply stands there, watching, makes each second stretch and snap into the next. Finally the shorts are underneath my ass and then on. I set the pillow aside, place my hands on the bed, and lean my weight back. More heavy breathing comes with a momentary relief.

"Now on to the pants," Garrett says. He looks around the room.

I hang my head; the pants are in the armoire. I need a break before this happens, but Garrett balks. I'm sure he wants this over as much as I do. I convince him to wait a bit.

He leans against the chest of drawers, texting with Noelle, his girlfriend whose name I'd been reminded of moments ago. I think about suffering through a conversation with her later, the pity she may express. Garrett's brow is creased in concern as he looks at his phone. I wonder if his news is about marriage, however unlikely that seems.

"Now that I'm wearing underwear, I need to ask you the real favor," I say.

Garrett drops the phone at his side, grins expectantly. "I didn't sign up to be your full-time home health aide."

His hoodies always make him seem young to me, the drawstrings begging to be yoked. He's never dressed fully like an adult—no collars or visible belts—not even as a thirty-year-old. "I wrote a speech for Lisa," I say, "and I can't read it."

He looks confused, like I lost the ability to read altogether.

"I mean every time I read it out loud, I can't."

"Your voice?"

"No." I falter. "My emotions get the best of me. I can't manage to keep it together."

Garrett looks surprised. "Not a thing I'd ever imagine you saying," he says. He thinks to himself for a second. "So you want me to read it?"

I nod.

"That feels a little weird, doesn't it?"

"You're reading it to the room. And I'd stand right there, next to you. You're like an interpreter, they'll barely notice you."

He rubs the scruff along his jaw. Is he planning to shave for the wedding?

"There's no one else I can ask," I say. "People will understand why you're doing it for me."

Garrett stands, silently mulling. "Can I see it?" he asks.

I nod at the papers near him. He grabs and unfolds them, and I watch his eyes scanning the first line. He peels the pages apart, and the corner of the top one falls to graze the one below. I've forgotten much of what I'd written about Lisa, or tried not to think about it too hard, but I make out the word *grandfather*, written in my slanted scrawl. I remember the part where I imagined her future kids.

"Wow," he says. "*Lisa's expansive kindness has taught me, beyond all else, about my own capacity to love.* Who knew you were such a writer."

I suddenly feel naïve, exposed.

"We're sure this is about *Lisa* Lisa?" He continues reading for a moment. "It's quite the ode."

I feel stuck where I am, or maybe on my back foot. I think Garrett knows this. "It has to be a grand gesture; don't give me that shit."

"I'm not sure how I feel about being your ventriloquist dummy."

"This isn't about you, Garrett. Please."

"It is though," he says. "In a way."

I remember when Garrett was up visiting me once, he must've been fourteen or so. Early days. Lisa was nine. At the time, Lisa liked to call Garrett her brother; she loved the idea of having one. Garrett felt the need to correct her, explaining what *step* meant, and Lisa quickly latched onto the word *step*, repeating it back in his face (I figured he needed to express himself to ever fully accept the new family). He'd never been tall, and Lisa had just grown several inches so was only a head or so shorter than he was. I was in the kitchen cooking when Garrett playfully wrestled her to the ground. He placed a foot on her stomach, asking if she knew what kind of *step* this was. I'd warned them to calm down, but it seemed harmless to me. Cute, even. Garrett then grabbed my half-drunk beer bottle from the edge of the kitchen island. A lime was floating in it. He held it over her head, incrementally tilting. I truly didn't think he'd spill it. I don't think he thought he'd spill it either. She screamed when the liquid hit her face, really not much at all. Garrett looked shocked and Teresa rushed into the kitchen to calm her down, asking what had happened. I told her they were messing around and she glared at me. Later I acted dismayed by what Garrett had done, but I felt little sympathy for Lisa. She was a nuisance and, besides, she was overreacting for effect—especially when her mom showed up. I've never understood my allegiance to Garrett so clearly as I did then.

After several minutes of standing, I'm tired. I sit slowly back down on the bed. "I've come through for you time and again, Garrett," I say. "Let me lean on you for once?"

"On cue," he says. "Lord the money over my head."

Lording is not how it works. The fact that he's needed me financially, and I've provided, is our unspoken contract. A bonding agent we're both dependent on. It constitutes as much of our relationship as anything else at this point. His referencing it feels like a betrayal.

"What I'm saying is that you're in a position to help me out. I'm not . . ." I trail off. I'd never needed Garrett to bail me out in this way. It feels important, or at least new. But I refuse to beg him for anything.

It's time for the pants, I decide. Garrett gets them from the armoire and brings them over. It's not as difficult as I'd imagined. He slides them up my calves, to my knees, and helps me stand straight up and put them on. I tell him we might as well do the socks now too. Get it over with. He brings them from the drawer as I sit back down. We should've done this part first, I think. I feel infantile with my legs hanging off the bed. He kneels again, sliding the thin black cotton onto my feet. I remember when he was little, putting his socks on had been such a satisfying action for me, the way he'd gently guide his toes inside. Then all at once, I start laughing. A force from deep in my gut. My face must look crazed because Garrett is bewildered. "What?" he asks, looking up at me. To imagine an explanation adds to the absurdity and only makes me laugh harder. How had I spent the last eight weeks meticulously building strength only to be incapacitated on the edge of the bed like a fucking toddler? And I mean I've never laughed like this. I'm whooping and squealing. It hurts in my hips, my back, but I can't stop. The pain adds its own current to the laughter.

I lean forward slightly, and tears fall on my pants. Garrett gets up and sits next to me on the bed. I feel the urge to clarify that I'm laughing and not crying, but I can't get ahold of the words. He laughs briefly, through his nose. He's never seen me cry, and I can feel his unease. But I'm laughing so hard I'm losing breath, or might stop breathing altogether. It feels like something slipped free from my grasp and I'm trying to catch it.

I button and unbutton my blazer, which, I gather from the mirror, will need an iron before we head down to the reception. My curly gray hair is flattened on the side from lying on the bed, and my face is splotched with pink. I've looked better. "You said you wanted to talk," I say.

I notice Garrett's thumbnail against the maple wood, chewed to a pulp. He crosses his legs. "Mom said I should wait—I'm not sure why I mentioned it earlier."

Of course he'd conferred with her. I try to take a step, but I'm unsteady. I want to walk to the window, to walk anywhere for a view to elsewhere. The inability is maddening. My hands are fists. It's like Garrett's finally got me trapped.

"So you ignored her advice for once," I say. The snipes are always loaded.

"Don't make this about her," he says.

Garrett has spent his entire life with his mother eagerly in his ear, but I've long accepted the necessity of keeping him in the dark to protect their relationship. How could I have ever told him she'd fallen in love with someone else? I remember crying one of the first nights in my shitty sublet, like I felt myself pushing the tears out, as if I was trying to get the dead car of my sadness moving in order to watch it roll away. Funny thing is, after six months, Garrett's mother said she'd made a mistake—she'd mistaken someone's attention for love—and wanted to fix things with me. I swear I nearly fell into her arms. The relief seemed at first like I was being saved from something, but then I'd taken a beat. Once her words settled, my relief hardened into something else. I told her I needed time. Then soon after I told her no; I was leaving. I had decided to believe in myself.

Garrett walks to the window and pulls apart the heavy curtain to peek outside. The sky is bright behind him, and he flattens to a silhouette.

I'm sitting back down on the bed, a relief I feel most immediately in my hips.

"Noelle is pregnant," he says.

I think I've misheard him. Had I not been sitting, I wonder how my shock would've manifested. I stare, trying to catch his gaze. "Garrett, that's great." My comment almost rises to a question.

He looks to the floor.

I want to ask him the relevant follow-ups—Is it a boy or a girl? Will they get married?—but he interrupts my thoughts.

"I don't want it," he says.

The way he says *it*.

"She's getting an abortion."

I feel the urge to rise again, to go over to him. But I'll need his help to get there so I can't. "How long have you known?"

"The week before last."

"Do you not want kids with her, or full stop?"

We've never discussed kids before.

"I don't know. I just know I'm not ready."

"Do you love her?" I ask.

"I think so. I do." He finally looks at me. His eyes are welling slightly. "She wanted it at first. Or at least she was excited. My hesitation put a damper on it. I watched a light go out in her."

"It's OK to be conflicted," I say. I imagine Garrett, in his hoodie, pushing a stroller along the bank of a lake. I imagine him prideful, happy. I imagine the three of us.

"I've never felt fully like myself with anyone, but I do with her."

I think that this fact is related to Noelle's apparent skepticism of me, that Garrett's ambivalence about fatherhood was caused by me.

"I can't think of disappointing Noelle," he continues. "I don't want to lose her, but I don't want this to be the reason we're together. I want to make the choice from a place of confidence and stability."

"You know I'll help, Garrett—" I start.

"Jesus, that's not what I'm saying," he says. "Not everything's a ledger item."

I want to say that everything has a ledger, but I'm not sure I believe the thought.

"Emotional stability," he continues. "I don't want to ruin a kid's life because I'm unprepared. There's no way I won't fuck it up, and I don't want to damage someone like that."

I think he might cry. I can't abide the thought, and I'm not sure what to say. I hear a cart being wheeled past the door, the clang of silverware against a plate.

A moment later my phone buzzes on the nightstand. I'm suddenly reminded of what's ahead. I imagine Teresa is worried about me, but there's still an hour or so before I have to get downstairs. I wish I could reach the phone to muffle it.

Garrett notices and says he should go. I plead with him to stay, and he relents. I tell him how I'm glad he told me when he did, and he nods, despite himself. I tell him that the truth is no one's ever ready. Every parent fucks their kid up, it's only a matter of how. He shakes his head, unconvinced. I say I was terrified when his mom was pregnant with him. I'd gone through a month of extreme insomnia at the time, like I'd be lucky if I slept for four hours a night. And I had to hide this from his mom because she was dealing with sciatica, nausea, everything. I'd be in bed ruminating on all the ways I'd be incapable of supporting a family. Like I was lying next to the person—the two people—I was destined to fail. It was torture. It got to the point where I was sneaking out of the house because I couldn't bear tormenting myself. I realize, now, that I'd never told anyone this before, with any level of detail. Garrett's face has softened with what looks to me like expectation.

I started to take walks down to East Fairmont, I tell him, following the water, so at least then I was moving along with my thoughts and had a sense of control. One morning I was sitting on a bench when I saw a man pushing a stroller on the opposite side of the water. He looked much younger than I was, and it seemed like he was being slowly pulled, like he lacked any agency in what he was doing. But then he stopped suddenly. He locked the stroller at the edge of the grass and took his kid out. Must've only been a few months old. He cradled the baby like a football, and kneeled close to the water. The baby started to reach its hands out and the guy used his other arm to support and swing the baby over the water. I watched that tiny hand reaching and reaching and finally making contact with the surface. One swipe left the tiniest wake. It was like the baby was an extension of the man, like they weren't two people. I watched the ripples spread and settle and I swear they eventually reached the edge close to where I was sitting.

Garrett looks down again.

"I copied that guy once you were born." I smile to myself. "I used to take you down to the water all the time."

He's picking his lip now, one foot bobbing against the floor.

"You deepened the way I saw the world, Garrett. Immediately."

"I appreciate the sentiment, but I'm not ready."

I search his face for the young boy I'd moved away from all those years ago. I often forgot how rich those early years were, and now it seems unfair that he'd been too young to hold as many of the memories as I could.

Garrett seems nervous. He's pacing now. His arms are folded, like he's gathering his thoughts. Though I feel spiritually lighter having told him the story, I doubt how much purchase it has found.

"I think you should take some time before you decide," I say. "You don't have to make up your mind this minute."

It seems he doesn't hear me. He's distracted. "You remember the first time you took me to New York?" he asks, his eyes searching mine.

I haven't thought about that trip in some time, but I tense, pressing my hands together.

"I'm not sure I've ever felt as alone as I did that first night," he continues.

My stomach drops. "Garrett," I begin.

We'd ordered pizza and watched *Natural Born Killers* that night, which I knew his mother would hate. He'd fallen asleep on me, and I'd carried him off to his new bed. After a few hours, he'd called my name and came out to find me rising from the couch in my underwear, startled.

"You were with a woman," he says. "I could hear her laughing, moaning, from the bedroom." He turns away. "I'll never forget your face. Standing in your underwear beside the couch and acting like you'd been asleep. I'd never seen an adult look like they'd been caught."

The woman in question was Teresa, not that it matters now. At the time, I'd panicked, leading Garrett quickly back to bed. I told him I was just going to grab some water from the kitchen, hoping to help Teresa get out, but he refused to let go of my hand. We laid in bed until he fell asleep, which felt like hours. Teresa eventually snuck out before dawn, and I remember listening to the rhythm of Garrett's breathing. I'd been mesmerized by the way his fragile chest would rise and fall.

"I didn't realize you knew." My hands, which had curled into fists, loosen. I feel like I do in the hours after swimming laps, my lungs newly capable of drawing air.

"I hated being in that apartment," he says.

I remember not ever fully finishing his bedroom. "I realize now that was selfish."

Garrett looks at his phone again, and then up at the ceiling. "I've been in this room too long. I'm gonna go," he says finally.

I want to tell him that this memory of his will help him be a good father, that it might even be the central reason for it. This could be wisdom or selfishness. Maybe both. "OK," I say.

Once Garrett reaches the door, I decide I want to stay in the room, remaining sealed in after the door shuts behind him for as long as I can. I don't feel capable of dealing with the wedding and try to imagine what would happen if I stay put. But I don't hear a sound. A second later, he walks back into the room to the chest of drawers and grabs the pages of my speech. I prepare to watch him tear them to shreds, which I wouldn't blame him for. Instead, he folds them up and tucks them into the pocket of his hoodie. He doesn't say anything to me, or even look in my direction as he leaves. The door slams closed. I just sit there for a second before pushing myself up to stand. I feel dizzy, but it passes. Garrett will be caught by surprise when he reaches the last line of my speech, that I end it with him. I hope he won't look over at me, because if I haven't already started sobbing, that look may level me.

I wipe my hands through my hair and look around the room. The drapes are still peeled back from where he'd been standing, a sliver of sky beaming into the room from the window. I take one slow step toward it.

ACKNOWLEDGMENTS

I'd like to thank my daughter, Lilly, without whom I'd be only a fraction of myself. Marissa, thank you for loving me unflinchingly, and Lía, for sharing Marissa with me. And my family: Mom, Dad, Clare, and Min. Also my oldest friends: Sam, Dante, Nick, Lena, Rowan, and Seyon.

Yahdon, thank you for your uncompromising vision for this book, which was greater than mine ever was, and for being a tireless collaborator in making it. To Molly, my incomparable agent, thank you for steering me toward the subject matter and for not only helping bring a dream to bear, but refining what the dream was in the first place. And to Chris Brand: Your cover changed the way I understood my own book.

And finally, the innumerable people who read, edited, and supported my writing: Andrew Ridker, Daniel Smith, Sidik Fofana, Todd Portnowitz, Thomas Gebremedhin, Zain Khalid, Andrew Martin, Ann Hulbert, Maya Chung, Kat Hu, Sara Martin, Rav Grewal-Kök, and Adam Ross.